AF253270

# TROUNCE

# TROUNCE

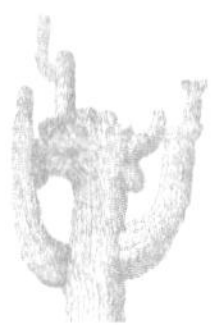

*George Beck*

*Full Court Press*
*Englewood Cliffs, New Jersey*

Published in the United States of America
by Full Court Press, 601 Palisade Avenue
Englewood Cliffs, NJ 07632

ISBN 978-0-578-01482-1
Library of Congress Control No. 2009924436

*Editing and Book Design by Barry Sheinkopf
for Bookshapers (www.bookshapers.com)*

*Colophon by Liz Sedlack*

*Cover by Anton Khodakovsky*

*Cover photo by David Shellor*

*What a man of you, having an hundred sheep, if he lose one of them, doth not leave the ninety and nine in the wilderness, and go after that which is lost, until he find?*

—Luke 15:4

CHAPTER 1

**W**E HAD ALREADY BEEN in the desert for two days. Lost. There seemed to be no relief from the merciless sun, not even a bit of shade to lie down in.

Arturo said we could cut open the barrel cactus and drink from it. I laughed humorlessly and said, "Go ahead, show me." He tried. It was foolish of him. He ended up pulling needles from his fingers and cursing everything but his mother.

He said half-heartedly, "If that truck hadn't gotten a flat when it did. . . ." That was how he was. He tended to blame all his ills on everything and everyone but himself. I can't tell you how often I asked myself why I'd agreed to go north with him. The money it cost me to pay the coyote was what I'd been saving to help my mother, to give her a better life.

Arturo was exhausted and overheated. Hell, I was, too. We

were both twenty-three and very desperate, lying like a pair of distressed dogs in a rock-strewn arroyo, leaning into the side that was mostly away from the sun. Everything we owned was wrapped up in our backpacks. It wasn't much. Earlier in the day we'd each had a half-full plastic jug of by-then very warm water. I'd kept warning him to go easy, but he was the type to want everything right now. I'd said, "The way you're drinking, man, you will die of thirst if we don't find someplace with water."

"I don't give a shit," he said.

There was very little water left in his jug, maybe a long swallow. I didn't say anything about it as we squatted there, our backs pressed into the cool rock where the sun hadn't touched. The rocks looked like they had been stained by old blood. I'd read in schoolbooks about the geology of that land—how the gringos had come and mined copper and raised plenty of hell in the old days and then when the copper ran out simply left everything and gone off. That's what I knew about southern gringos. They frightened me a little.

"We'll wait until the hottest part of the day has passed," I suggested. "Then keep going when the sun is setting."

"Who made you boss?" he said, trying to make a joke.

"Cut it out," I said.

Sometimes when we weren't joking with each other or teasing, we didn't have much to say. After we finished high school, I'd gone off to college and he'd stayed, drunk a lot of booze, and picked the pockets of gringos who came south for tourism. But, other than pick-pocketing, he hadn't done anything too terribly bad. Still, over the last few years we'd been going our separate ways, and I was pretty sure we'd become strangers one day.

I wanted to become a lawyer, to bring justice to those who needed it most, but it was hopeless—I couldn't find work. I had big dreams, and there I was sitting in a slash in the earth, pretty sure I was going to end up dead in the Arizona desert. It is one thing to die. It is another to die alone in a strange land.

But I wouldn't die completely alone. Arturo would die with me.

We waited another two or three hours and started out again. The land all looked the same, with cactus—the prickly pear and the big saguaros—the ocotillo, and off in the distance the feathery Palo Verde. Way in the distance you could see the jagged teeth of the gray mountains. But it was all pretty much the same.

We walked maybe a mile more then came across one red tennis shoe. We looked at each other.

Arturo chuckled. "Bastard lost his shoe."

"He must have been in a hurry," I said.

Arturo laughed.

"Bastard was running, eh."

"Yeah," I said. We moved on.

Through the last of the heat that shimmered up from the hardpan we spotted the lone house, the pipe corral, the outbuildings.

"You see that?" Arturo said.

"Yeah, I see it," I said.

"What do you think?"

"I think we should be careful. Vigilantes, remember?"

"Those bastards," he said.

We'd seen them on television, the Americans who called them-selves by various names and volunteered to protect the border even though their own government said they didn't want them there, to be armed and maybe shoot innocent people.  Such is the price of democracy:  People do pretty much what they want.

But our bellies were knotted with hunger and our water was running out and we felt desperate.

"Come on, Emilio.  If no one is home, we can sneak in.  We need food and fresh water."

"I'm not sure."

He flashed the back of his hand to me.  "I feel *sick*.  I need to *eat*," he said.  "It may be days before we reach Phoenix.  Relax.  I'll just be a minute."

He laid his backpack by my feet.

*Whose fault was this?* I wanted to blurt out. *I told you so*, but in-stead, I said in a low voice, "I'll stay here and stand guard, okay?  If you hear me whistle, get out of there as fast as you can!"

"Emilio, we need this."

I didn't say anything.

"You came here to help your sick mother back home, right?  If we die, what's the point?"

"Yeah," I said, "but this isn't right, Arturo!"

"You tell me what's right?  Is it right we die in the middle of nowhere?  Just wait here, and I'll bring us back something to eat."

I shrugged.  "Stay quiet."

Every instinct in my body told me that my return into America had been a bad idea.  Seven years before, my father and I'd got

picked up by ICE and been sent back to the land of the Maya with

stern instructions to "never return."

I inhaled the hot air and wiped my forehead with my sleeve.

Off in the distance, I heard the distant thunder of hoofbeats and

the lowing of cattle.

I watched him sneak toward the place, bent over, going back and

forth, trying to hide himself behind the little cactus and scrub.  It

was foolish, I thought.  If somebody was inside that house watching,

they'd spot him easily and know he was up to no good because of

the way he was sneaking around.  *Cabron,* I thought.

His blue cowboy shirt with the pearl buttons had come out of

his greasy jeans, and his old tennis shoes were frayed and dirty.  He

looked like what he was— what they call an illegal.

I saw him pause at the horse corral.  There were no horses in

it.  Then he came around the end toward the house, which was

nothing more than some old green trailer that somebody had added

onto piece by piece until they had something more than a trailer

and less than a real house.  There was also a small shed a few dozen

yards to the east, its corrugated tin roof streaked with rust.

I called out, "Arturo, be careful.  Vigilantes, remember?"

"Bullshit, Emilio!"

Arturo got up to where a window was and tried looking in.  It

was dark and dirty.  Then he looked back to where I was squatting

and waved for me to come on.  I didn't want to.  But I went anyway,

thinking at least maybe we could get some fresh water.

My eyes were riveted on Arturo as he stood at the window. I saw the muscles of his shoulder bulge; then, with a herculean effort, he forced open the window. He had begun pulling himself in when a horrifying scream chilled my blood. *"Arturo!"* I screamed. The place looked empty. He was hanging out of the window, his legs kicking madly.

"Help! Oh, my *God*! *Help* me, Emilio!"

From inside the house, I heard the ferocious growl of a dog. Arturo continued to scream as he tried backing out of that window—but he must have gotten caught on something. He couldn't free himself. The growl had me frozen. I didn't know what to do.

"Emilio, *help* me! *Help me!"* he screamed again. It tore at me. *"Help me! Emilio!"*

I never should've returned. He was going to get us both caught. But a shot of guilt ran through my body. I stomped my foot, clenching both straps on my backpack, took a deep breath, and ran toward him. I was going to get him loose, and then we were out of there. If he couldn't keep up, at least I could say that I hadn't left him to die. I was not thinking these things: I was breathing them.

The dog was attacking him. I yanked him back by his ankles as hard as I could, tearing his shirt on the sill. The dog let go. Arturo fell back onto me, and we crashed on the dirt with a loud thud. Arturo groaned. He was bleeding badly. Whatever it was that had torn his shirt had also dug a long, open wound into his abdomen. It looked like it had been filleted with a sharp knife. Wet blood was saturating the clothing.

The dog leaped wildly at the sill, unable to get out, its snarl terrifying. It then began barking, stripping its teeth, trying again to jump out of the window.

"Let's *go!*" I screamed. "We can find a town where someone can help."

I got up, but he didn't. He covered his bloody face with his hands and couldn't suppress the scream that came next. I tore off his shirt and tied it around his abdomen, to stop the bleeding, and silently whispered, *Lord, please help me.* I lifted him, my back straining as I hefted him over my shoulders and lugged him away from the house. His blood was dripping down my shirt and onto my jeans like the blood of a slaughtered cow.

As we neared the end of the driveway, we stumbled into a man on a horse.

"What the hell?" he blurted.

I froze like a deer in a truck's headlights.

"Jesus *Christ!*" he swore.

The man had dismounted, tied his horse to a hitching post, and was heading toward us.

He was a massive guy with an unkempt red beard and red hair spilling out of a black Stetson. He was tall, rangy, and looked about fifty years old, but his shoulders were wide. For some reason, I noticed the spurs on his russet, steel-tipped boots were worn and his jeans dusty. And his lifeless eyes.

I caught the sun's reflection on the chrome of the revolver holstered on his hip.

"Damn thieving illegals on my property," he drawled. "What

the hell are you doing here?"

I took a step backward, tripped, and fell to my side in the dust, dropping Arturo to the ground. "Sir," I cried out, "we didn't do any harm. We needed fresh water." I scrambled to my feet, hands up.

"I could give a shit. You wetbacks are all the same. Damn thieves! I'm glad my dog got you!"

Frozen, I began to see white. Just then his horse made a sound, and he looked over to it. I sprinted off as fast as I could, leaving Arturo rolling around at the man's feet, muttering now like a baby. After a short distance I threw myself behind a stand of brush to see what was going on.

I saw the backswing of the man's right leg and how it flashed forward, the steel tip of his boot chiseling into Arturo's side. I heard him scream through his teeth.

I wanted to get up and run some more, but there was a part of me that had to see. My chest was pumping in a panic. I saw the man holding Arturo's floppy body halfway up. Arturo's legs sprawled out along the ground like a punch-drunk boxer's leaning against the ropes, his bloody hair threaded between the fingers of the man, who had his back to me and was bending in, as if he was speaking to him. The dog had at last freed itself from the house and was lunging at Arturo's legs.

I stayed crouched out of sight. I took a deep breath, trying to slow my mind while my heart pounded rapidly. I was terrified and shaking. Sweat burned my eyes. *What was he telling Arturo?*

I hoped that Arturo would free himself, but in his state, how could he? He was hurt, and I knew he couldn't run. Then I saw a metallic glint and knew it was the man's pistol as the dog continued attacking. I closed my eyes and prayed. The shot rang out and echoed in the distance. There was a brief stillness through which the wild barking of the dog persisted.

*Oh my God! He killed Arturo—oh my God!* A surge of anger and sorrow burst through my veins as if someone was pulling me from both poles. I felt like running back there and snatching that gun, turning it on him, and evening the score. I wanted to savor the smell of gunpowder while I avenged Arturo's death. But I had no weapon. Or the nerve.

The man stepped away from Arturo and started for his horse. I began running as fast as I could. I knew I had to make real distance from him. I knew he would try to hunt me on horseback with his dog on my trail. I dove into the heavy brush along a dried up river-bank and began working my way into the thickness of it.

I heard the barking of the dog and the approaching thunder of hooves. I kept pulling my way in toward the middle of the heavy brush as quietly as possible. I had no choice. If he found me, I knew he would kill me.

For some reason he must have veered off in another direction. I sensed this because the dog's barking faded off into the distance. I lay deep in the heavy brush, praying that God would keep him from finding me.

Then the barking was no more. I bolted out of the brush and ran until I found a small town a few miles east called Beyerville. It set me off course, but when I saw the peaks of the houses way in the distance, I sprinted straight to them. In minutes I was hiding in a metal shed behind a wooden shack. I wasn't sure if the red-bearded man had called the police and given them my description, and I didn't want to take the chance of getting caught, so I crept into a sheltered space behind a lawnmower and gardening tools.

Time stood still. I began to think over the last few days. It'd cost six thousand American dollars, of which I only paid a down payment of one thousand, to have a coyote sneak me into the country, and well worth it until the day before, when the van, in which Arturo and I were packed like livestock with twelve others, got a flat tire.

The elderly Mexican driver had pulled over, looking terrified as he sat tapping the steering wheel with an index finger, his eyes glued out the side-view mirror as his partner, who sat with him in the front seat, got out to change the tire. It'd been so quiet you could hear the whirr of the desert flies. The heat had grown more and more intense by the minute. Soon after, the distant *whoop* of a police car had shattered the silence.

"*Correr!*" the driver had shouted. "*Run!*"

We'd jumped out, scurrying in all directions like cockroaches under a light. I'd run so fast, I nearly collapsed. Arturo had kept up with me. Almost twenty minutes later, we had stopped and scanned the area for pursuing cops. There were none, and we'd sat down, panting like wolves.

Now Arturo was dead.

It was unnerving in the shed. At nightfall, I snuck out and continued north.

CHAPTER **2**

THE TRIP ACROSS THE desert was sheer hell.  I walked at night to avoid the blistering sun.  During the day I found any bit of shade I could—a cactus, an outcropping of rock, anything.  There I lay up like the snakes and Gila monsters hiding from the sun, and thought of Arturo.  I wept for him and for myself.  I ate mesquite beans and cactus pears.  There was some juice in them.  It was the only liquid I had left after the plastic bottle I had found in the shed and filled with water was all gone.  In the mornings before the sun came up, I licked dry every leaf I could find.  I made sure I was in an area with some vegetation for just this purpose.

In the end it took five days across that unforgiving desert, but I survived the journey to Phoenix.

The rain was dancing along the streets when I got there around eight in the evening. I found a water fountain, thrust my parched tongue into the water, and began lapping like a dying dog. At last, I took a deep breath and raised my face to the sky. I guess I looked like a madman. The city was crowded with people tucked under umbrellas, walking to and from restaurants, shops, and the active nightlife of a big city.

After my thirst, my hunger was severe, a living thing twisting in my belly. My legs had grown heavy as stone. I had begun to lose faith and sworn that I was going to pass out and die alone in the middle of nowhere. Nobody would have known. Or if they had, would they have actually cared for another Salvadorian stampeding across the border into their country? I didn't think so.

I remembered hearing that the transfer point where my van should be waiting for me was at Central Station, in Cooper Square, the downtown section of the city. After holding my hands out to about twenty fast-moving people as if I were begging for money and pleading with them for directions, someone finally told me how to get there.

I made my way through a steady stream of people who all seemed to be in a serious hurry. For all that I heard about the American South Westerner being laid back and slow paced, I found them completely the opposite, at least the city people. Nobody had a minute to stop and talk with me. They just waved fingers in the right direction and continued on. No one even looked me in the eye. I guess they had seen many men of my kind passing through and considered us another kind of weed, an outgrowth in the cracks of the sidewalk. It didn't bother me. They were simply industrious folks with problems like mine, only they consumed themselves with their own lives.

As I neared Cooper Square, I prayed a van would be there, that the driver would be waiting for stragglers. I passed a train and at last was standing at Central Station. Tall buildings, and lots of concrete and polished glass, surrounded it. There was a twisted metal sculpture in front of one of the buildings. Amid the façade of modern beauty, however, I smelled the sewer system—a heavy, pungent odor in the air—clogged by more falling rain than it could handle.

I was tired and sat precariously on a wet bench outside the terminal. A sea of buses flowed past, throwing waves of rainwater over the curb, soaking my already drenched sneakers. There was no van waiting. It must have been long gone. *What do I do?* I thought, and sat there. At one point I realized that I had my head in my hands, and I pulled myself together. I didn't care to look *that* pathetic.

Arturo was dead, and my money was wasted because of that single flat tire that had now destroyed the next leg of my trip — Phoenix to Los Angeles. When you retain a coyote, he coordinates and makes the connections for you. A good coyote with the right links can get you to New Jersey in two weeks. A bad one can sometimes take longer than a month. Trust my luck to be saddled with one whose van had lousy tires. I wondered how long it would take me to get to where I was headed. A lifetime?

I knew I had to make it to Los Angeles somehow, to meet up with the coyote. I had to get aboard one of the daily vans he used to transport a bulk of men across the country. Los Angeles was a major transfer point; it was where a lot of men gave up and started looking for work.

I sat and thought of how nice it would be to be in New Jersey and to start making money to wire back home for Momma.

And then I was thinking again about Arturo. Never could get him out of my mind. I wept deeply, silently for nearly twenty minutes. It seemed as if my life was falling apart. I'd never imagined my life would implode so fast. For all that Arturo hadn't been, he was one thing: dead.

The year before, when I spent a weekend home from college, Arturo and I had gone to a salsa dance contest. He was the life of the party, with his tight jeans, collared shirt, straw cowboy hat, and crooked smile. Arturo was a great dancer. He had a natural ability to move effortlessly. The crowd knew it because at the end of the night they voted him best dancer, an honor he felt everybody in the world should be aware of.

I wondered how I would tell his mother. Would she blame me for his death? I had been there and done nothing to save him. Then again, only *I* knew that.

I felt helpless and dangerously desperate. The feeling was like a pain in my chest. . .but maybe it was only hunger. I was hungry like I never was before. Poppa once told me you could get a man to do almost anything when he can touch his spine through his stomach. Without a solid meal for five days, my head had started to get fuzzy. I had to find food.

I got up weakly and started down the street. I told myself there would be some sort of restaurant, and that restaurants do dump good food. I was in luck. Just around the block from Central Station I spotted a Mexican place. I slipped past the front of it and found myself at the back, where there were garbage cans and a large dumpster. I approached it and was lifting the lid when I smelled tobacco and, a moment later, heard a voice. "Hungry, *amigo?*"

I turned, too weak to be startled, and saw a short, squat man in a dirty apron sitting on a crate by a rear door. In one hand he had a cigarette, in the other, a partly-eaten foot-long sandwich. There was a soda by his feet.

"Yes," I whispered, nodding.

"Here," he said, holding out the sandwich.

I took it. "You can take this too. . ." He held out the soda. I took it too, and thanked him. He turned without a further word and disappeared inside.

I sat on the crate and devoured half of the sandwich. I rewrapped the other half in the greaseproof paper and stuck it into my backpack. I drank off the soda and started roaming through the streets.

The city grew darker. Rain clouds were scuttling across the moon. A Phoenix P.D. patrol car drove past, and it got me thinking. I had a choice to make. I could call Arturo's murder to the police's attention and tell them what I had seen. But then I considered what the police would say. After all, I was an illegal alien—or, as I preferred to be called, an undocumented immigrant. And what if the red-bearded man had reported Arturo's death, claiming he had killed him in self-defense because he tried to rob his house? Then

I would become an accomplice. This would most likely get me jailed, which would only hurt my mother. Still, I felt the police needed to know the truth. As the squad car turned a corner, I decided there *had* to be another way, one that didn't involve me speaking directly with them.

Through all of my sorrow, I had to remember that Arturo was dead, and there was nothing I could do to bring him back to life. But my mother was still alive, fighting for her life. I had to concentrate on getting enough money to send home for her cancer treatments and pay the coyote off within one year. We hadn't had the money for him, so we'd given him a down payment, and Poppa had given a lien against our coffee farm for the rest of the money. I had to somehow make money fast enough to pay for both.

My mother had taught me that family was the most important part of life. We each had to do our best to help each other. She always put us ahead of her health problems. Even after she was diagnosed with skin cancer seven years before, the legacy of years of Central American sun, she had disregarded it and focused on providing for us, and up until recently left her cancer untreated. Aware she had it, without any money for medicine, she had prayed that God would either heal her or bring her home.

In its early stages, the cancer had been confined, mostly, to her upper back and neck. Then, she'd been hopeful things would get better for her with regular medication. Her positive outlook, however, had evaporated when it began to spread and the pain worsened. Our family doctor had said there was a long shot, a chance that she would be able to survive, but she needed an oncologist to administer a progressive new treatment, which included pills only a pharmacist could pronounce, and, of course, the ability to pay for it. But where would we get the money? We were poor, and I had known then and there that I would have to come to the States to make the money for her.

I was thinking about all the missed years I'd spent away from my mother. I'd left her when I was seven. Dad had sneaked me into the States with him. We had settled in the northeastern corner of New Jersey, just outside New York City, a lucrative land within a stone's throw of the Hudson River called Union City. At eight, I had been placed in the third grade, where I stayed until eleventh grade—sixteen and a year shy of graduating when we got the boot.

Now I was on my way back.

As I grew up, she and I had talked weekly on the telephone. And if we hadn't gotten thrown out, I doubt Poppa would have left so soon. He'd been making good money painting houses, sending home enough money for Momma and his sister, my Aunt Gloria— enough to put Aunt Gloria through college.

The rain was getting heavier, thunder rolling in the distance. I had nowhere to be, so I continued walking, trying to figure out how much I needed to make a week. I knew if I worked for a con- tractor in New Jersey, I could probably pull in six hundred Amer- ican dollars a week. At that rate, I could pay the coyote and still have enough money for Momma—or at least I hoped.

It was getting late, and I didn't want to spend the night out in the open, on the wet sidewalk, so I kept roaming the streets looking for a place to stretch out. I was searching for a spot to cover me from the rain where I thought I could be reasonably safe.

After almost a half-hour more of wandering, I saw a sign that was pointing to *Barrios Unidos Park*.

Deep into the park, I found a stand of trees in a shaded area. Off to the east stood an amphitheater, a playground, basketball court, and ball fields. It was a peaceful place where I could hang out without arousing suspicion; but mostly I wanted to sleep.

I found a park bench under the shade of a big tree and stretched out with my backpack as a pillow under my head. The rain continued, dripping through the leaves and branches for most of the night.

I woke in the early morning to the sounds of birds singing and the blazing warmth of the sun, and ate the last of the sandwich. I then stretched and continued to lie in the sunshine. I thought a lot. I had to somehow find a way to get some money for food, so I set out, found a garbage container, and fished an old coffee cup out of it. I was going to use it to collect coins on the street. I had a change of clothes in my backpack, but I kept on my rain-beaten, sun-dried ones. For what I was going to do next, I needed my desperation to be obvious.

I found a busy office building, stood before it, and panhandled for most of the morning. By late afternoon, I had a little more than fifteen dollars in change and a few dollar bills.

I knew I should try to stretch my food money out as long as possible, but the five days of starvation had affected me worse than I realized. Still, even fast food would make the money go quickly, so I found a grocery store and bought a can of spaghetti and meatballs. That would be lunch and two cans of beef stew for dinner and breakfast. For a little over two dollars I had taken care of food for the day and the morning. I bought the kind of cans with a pull-off top and a package of plastic spoons.

Back at the park I ate the spaghetti. Nothing had ever tasted so good. Again I stretched out on the park bench, but my mind was too busy for sleep. I sat up and pulled out a pack of small cigars a man with a suit had tossed me earlier, feeling, I guess, that I needed a smoke more than the change I was shaking my cup for. Nothing like a smoke after a meal: It helped me think.

With night approaching I again had to find someplace to sleep. I knew if I stayed on the same bench, chances were the cops would pick me up for vagrancy. I wanted no encounters with cops. I couldn't take the chance. If I kept moving around, I would be less likely to be picked up, so I wandered the streets of Phoenix, hunting for someplace to bunk down for the night.

I must have looked needy, because I was approached by a kid. He couldn't have been more than fifteen. His dark skin and pine fine black hair suggested he was Hispanic, and his short stature and slanted eyes had the look of the Mayan. He looked tentative when he approached me. "Hey, man, you got a cigarette?"

I was about to say no when I remembered the cigars. I dug one out of my pocket and said, "It's all I have."

He reached for it and said, "*Gracias.*"

He dug into the pocket of a threadbare shirt, took out a book of matches, and lit up. I started walking. He came after me. "You got someplace to sleep?"

"No," I said, eyeing him. I didn't want to get mugged, and by then I was pretty paranoid.

"I got me a place. It looks like rain tonight. You need a roof, man."

"Where is the place?"

He grinned. "You come with me."

By the time he led us to his home under a bridge, I had learned that his name was Pedro, that he was fifteen, and, like me, that he had come from El Salvador. I asked him from where exactly.

"Acajutla." He seemed sad when he said it.

"Ah, Acajutla. Beautiful beaches. What do your folks do for work?"

"Ah," he said grinning. "We work for the *padrone* mostly. That and any odd jobs we can pick up. . . . Where you from?"

"Tenancingo. It's near San Salvador."

"Yes," he said. "Beautiful place. Nice and cool."

Sure enough, we no sooner got settled on some cardboard and rags he used for a bed than it started to rain. That bridge became a solid refuge in that deluge.

It was almost dark when I fished out my can of beef stew. He didn't seem to have anything to eat, so I offered him the other can, which he gratefully accepted. "*Gracias, gracias,*" he mumbled.

We ate the stew as if it were a gourmet dinner. Afterwards we smoked. He had kept half of the cigar I'd given him.

I asked, "What's your plan here in Phoenix?"

"Get a job, man. Send some money home."

"Have you had any luck?"

"Not much. If you don't get anything steady, you wind up using the little money you have, and it is tough out here, man. You got to watch everybody. Everybody out here steals from you."

I looked at him. "Why do you trust me?"

He hesitated. "Something about the eyes, man. Besides, you're doing all the giving. I can tell from people's eyes if they're good or not. My momma taught me that."

Considering my recent behavior, that remark made me feel good, though guilty at the same time. I thought again of Arturo and how I hadn't reported his murder or avenged his death. And there was something about Pedro that got me thinking more about my purpose for being in America. I had come solely to help my mother, but I wondered if there was a way I could help Arturo's mother, too. She would need justice. Somehow, I had to find a way to accomplish both. Eventually I got tired of thinking. I laid on a frown and started to get depressed.

Off to the west, thunder rumbled again. Grateful to be covered and reasonably fed for the day, I listened to the heavy downpour on the pavement outside the bridge. It didn't take long for Pedro to fall asleep. He seemed to be comfortable in his makeshift home. I, too, tried to get comfortable and fall asleep.

I rolled over a few times. But when I closed my eyes, there he was: the red-bearded rancher who had shot my friend. I heard him laughing and swore he was stalking me from the corner of the bridge, his cruel eyes blazing at me. I was on my hands and knees, panting, bracing myself for an attack and kept looking around furtively, expecting to be blindsided.

The anxiety lasted until I forced myself to believe that it was only in my mind. I needed to get some rest. My heart was beating fast as I closed my eyes again, praying the Lord could ease my anxiety and help me fall asleep. I was exhausted and wanted to be home with my parents. No matter what I tried to tell myself, I could still hear that man's voice, and it terrified me through the night.

CHAPTER **3**

**B**Y MORNING THE RAIN had stopped. I hadn't slept well on the cardboard, huddled up in my flannel, waking up every half hour expecting to find Arturo's killer standing over me. I was terrified, and the creepiness of squatting under a bridge made things that much worse.

During the middle of the night I heard a dog howl, and I froze, again terrified I'd see the killer and his dog. I knew he wanted me dead, and that somehow I'd escaped. I stared into the darkness and wondered what the man had thought the other day when he couldn't find me.

I sighed and shook my head, figuring he'd maybe shrugged it off and gone back home with his dog. Maybe he'd told himself that I was just a wetback who'd be too scared to go to the police. I was pretty sure he'd come up with a story to make it seem Arturo had attacked him, or something—dead men don't offer testimony. I thought of the squad car I'd seen the day before and was glad I hadn't reported the incident.

I knew I had to get back to sleep, so after thirty minutes of listening to the distant barking of that dog, I finally drifted off.

The rising sun was red, foretelling another hot day. I shook my head, thought of the night before, realized how illogically I had been acting, and smiled grimly. The chances of that killer finding me sleeping on cardboard under a bridge in Phoenix were remote. I had to steer my thoughts away from him, but I couldn't.

"What are you going to do today, *mi amigo*?" It was Pedro.

"Organize my head," I said, "and try to make a move out of here."

"I'm going to cool out a little bit longer," he said, yawning, and settled back on to his cardboard.

"I'll see you when I see you, Pedro." I grabbed my stuff together. "And thanks for the help."

"Where you going now?" he asked.

"I'll be in that park a while."

I spent the morning sitting in Barrios Unidos, dozing and watching the kids play on the grass. About noon, Pedro came by. "Hey, man. I got me a job sweeping the church courtyard and washing the floors in the rectory. You want to come along? Help me a bit, and the padre will give us a meal."

What else did I have to do? I went along.

The padre was a short, round priest with kind eyes whom Pedro introduced as Father Georgio, and after we did the work, he sat us down in a small back room and had the maid serve us a meal from a small eat-in kitchen.  I was about to dig in when Father Georgio's eyes caught mine.  He bowed his head, and Pedro and I did, too.  After a brief blessing, we picked up our forks.  It was meatloaf, macaroni and cheese, Italian bread with butter, and coffee.  My shrunken stomach almost burst from the size of that meal.

If nothing else I was learning the ways of the vagabond, which were coming in handy as I waited to schedule a meeting with the coyote.  I knew I would have to call home and have Poppa arrange it for me, but I wasn't sure if now was the right time to spend the little money I had on a phone card.  I had to keep what I had left for food and water.  I figured I'd wait to see how much money I could make panhandling again.

So I found myself back with Pedro under the bridge that night. We built a small campfire and sat around smoking and drinking coffee he had made from the battered old coffeepot among his things. As a stream of smoke departed his thin lips, he told me, "I love my coffee, man. We grow it back home, and I've been drinking it since I been a kid."

I said, "Do you really think you have a chance of finding work?"

"I don't know, man.  I hope."

"But, Pedro, you have no address where you live, no papers, no ID.  How can you possibly make it?"

He smiled sadly. "Others have done it, man.  Besides, what else can I do? There is no work at all back home.  I got to get money to my family somehow. I heard of a man looking for fruit pickers west of here. He'll be around in a couple days where some of the other illegals hang out. I was hoping to get some work."

"But what then?"

"Don't know, man. One day at a time."

"Why you alone?" I asked.

"Been alone since last year, man. But, I don't want to talk about it."

I was no psychologist, but I thought that Pedro needed to talk, so I pressed on. "You came here since last year?"

It took a while for him to answer, and I sensed he was getting upset, so I was just about to let it go when a cool breeze swept under the bridge, kicking up some trash. It seemed to remind us both of our miserable situation. "You think I want to live here like *this?*" he said.

I didn't respond. There was no point.

"I was left stranded. My father died last year. Construction accident. Horrible, man. He fell down fourteen floors."

I was taken back. I mean, I knew there was a reason why a young kid was homeless, but I hadn't expected that.

"We had a nice place. One day he didn't come home, so I waited three days, then went to the *policia*. You know, they took me to the hospital and I identified his body. I'll never forget not wanting to see the face covered by that sheet."

Pedro was crying, and it gave me goose bumps. I put my arm around his shoulders.

"Thank God for that kind doctor—*con la moneda, sabes*," he said, rubbing two fingers together, his voice breaking. "He paid to send him home to my mother for burial."

"What about you? Why didn't you go?"

He wiped his tears with the back of his hand. "What for? I wanted to make some money. It was why my father died."

"I wish there was a way I could help you."

"No, man, I'll make it," he said and shook my hands off from his shoulders. "You can't worry about me, *mi amigo.* You have to take care of yourself."

The next morning, Pedro grabbed a pail and a couple of squeegees he had secreted on a ledge under the bridge and said, "We make some *centivos* today, man."

I looked puzzled. He said, "I show you. But first we need a bath."

I had forgotten all about personal hygiene, and I just now realized how grungy I felt.

Pedro and I walked to a McDonald's and went into the washroom. We gave ourselves a cat bath with soap and hot water, washing to the waistline. Then we wet a towel with soapy water and one with clear water, went into the bathroom stalls and finished. I put on a fresh pair of blue jeans, a white T-shirt, and a windbreaker I carried with me in my backpack. We had to hurry, since the employees would chase us out if they caught us. Luckily, they weren't paying attention. After that I shaved with a disposable plastic razor I had bought and felt like a new man.

We both had an Egg McMuffin and a coffee and set out to work.

Pedro picked out an intersection of Seventh Street and Washington, right outside a big building with a sign that read *Phoenix Civic Center*. There were some other homeless people there with the same idea. Pedro said, "Sooner or later the cops will move us. We don't give them no hassle, man, *comprende?* We don't want no trouble with the cops."

The operation was simple. You just walked up to a car stopped at the red light, smiled, and started to wash the windshields. Some protested and closed their windows. Others said nothing, just drove off when the light turned green. Still others handed us a dollar bill.

Of course, we took the opportunity to indulge in women watching. I was leaning over, doing a windshield, when I spotted a pair of sleek, gorgeous legs, skirt up to the thighs, that belonged to a beautiful gringa in dark sunglasses. She spotted me looking and smiled. She had very white teeth.

Just then Pedro came over to the car, and she rolled down the passenger side window. "Hey, boys," she called out.

Pedro said, "Ah, Miss Sara."

I was confused and gave Pedro a look. I couldn't see how he could have known such a gringa. I was thinking quickly. But I couldn't make the connection.

She said, "Baby, you and your handsome friend looking for work?"

"Yes, Miss Sara," Pedro said eagerly.

She was grinning when she tilted down her sunglasses, showing her piercing brown eyes. "Well, get in."

Pedro turned to me, his eyes full of excitement and whispered, "*Que haya mucho dinero, chico.*"

We slid into the back seat of that black BMW with jet black leather and an overpowering new car scent mixed with perfume. Sara was smiling at Pedro. She seemed fond of him. She said, "I need you to move some furniture. I'm leaving for San Francisco at the end of the week, and I can't manage it by myself. Thirty dollars each, okay?"

Pedro turned to me, nodding, "Yes, yes, Miss Sara. Thirty's good."

We drove a short distance to a tall apartment building that had a lot of windows that looked like it'd been built sometime in the past ten years. It had that modern look—new age art in the lobby, a front desk with uniformed employees, and a guy in a suit at the front door with a portable radio device clipped to his back pocket. "Good day. Welcome, Miss Buchanan," said the man in the suit.

Sara smiled and nodded. "Hey, Reggie."

We strolled through the lobby and into the elevator, where Sara pointed to the garage-level button. "There's the U-haul truck. It should be big enough."

"No problem," I said.

Her apartment had all the signs of someone wealthy. The kitchen was large, with a green granite island in the middle. The appliances were stainless steel and looked expensive. In the living room stood a huge plasma television, at least fifty inches wide, flanked by soft black leather couches and other trendy pieces. A mirror along one wall made the living room seem much larger.

The place was fashionable, and, judging from the weight of the furniture, her stuff was expensive.

Pedro and I had a dolly that we used to roll a chest to a freight elevator on the opposite side of the building and down into the parking garage.

"So, Pedro, how do you know her?"

"I've washed dishes at her restaurant. At least ten days this year."

"Fancy place?"

"Nah, it's small, man. But she does well."

"Why doesn't she hire you regularly?"

"She has steady workers. Mexicans. She gets me when tourism picks up. Forty dollars a day."

"That's it?"

Pedro smirked. "I stretch it out for two weeks."

We went back up.

"Take the couch next," Sara called out from the kitchen.

She was standing at the sink, rinsing some dishes. I stared at her for what felt like forever. She had long brown hair cut to a point in the middle of her back. Her short red floral-print dress hid none of her curves. Her legs were long and sleek, her calves tight, and her thighs. . .well, they were dreamy. She had a full figure and was, I guessed, at least two or three years older than me. My gawking must have been obvious, because Pedro slapped me in the arm. "Come on, man, you know we not getting paid by the hour."

"Okay, okay, just slide the dolly under when I say."

I had bent down and lifted it just enough for Pedro to slide the dolly under when it happened. I was staring again at Sara in the mirrored wall when I accidentally dropped the couch and the wooden leg pinned Pedro's hand into the floor.

"Aiee! *Aiee, ooooo!*" he shrieked.

Sara came running in with wet hands. "What happened?"

"Just a little accident," I said.

Pedro cried, "*Little accident?* I think it's *broke*, man. All because you're gazing at Miss Sara and not looking at what you're doing!"

"I'm sorry, man," I mumbled, embarrassed. But his hand did look as though it was broken. It was swelling fast, with hints of purple and blue blotching under the skin.

Sara moved quickly but confidently to the kitchen and came back with ice cubes in a plastic bag. "Keep this on his hand," she said to me.

As I did so, I noticed that the hand was getting bigger, nearly double the size of his other, and swelling like a hamburger bun. He was tearing a lot. "It hurts *bad*," he said, voice shaking.

Sara said, "Let's go," and grabbed her purse off a table in the living room. "To the hospital."

I put my arm around Pedro. "I'm sorry, *amigo*. It was an accident."

"I know, man, but it still *hurts.*"

We headed down to Sara's car.

Soon we were on the same street where we'd washed windshields. Shortly thereafter, I noticed a sign indicating that Arizona State Hospital's emergency room was ahead. It was difficult for her to find a spot to park, but she managed to squeeze into one pretty close to the Emergency Room entrance, right where three ambulances were idling in designated parking spots.

Outside the tinted automatic sliding glass door were a lot of people talking on cell phones. A young guy in a wheelchair was propelling his way out into the parking lot as we were walking in.

"It really hurts," Pedro whined.

"Okay, baby, we're here. They're going to fix it," Sara said.

Once inside the hospital we found ourselves among a lot of other people in the emergency waiting room. Sara stopped a middle-aged nurse walking past with a clipboard. "Excuse me, Ma'am," Sara said. The nurse turned. "My friend here has hurt his hand badly, can you tell me how long it may be before he sees a doctor?"

The nurse took a glance at Pedro's swollen hand. "I don't know," she said. "It's going to be a while." She looked up after giving Pedro's hand a cursory examination. "He's going to live, don't worry. Just sit and wait."

We sat in the waiting room with people who had similar injuries, kids who were crying and a few young people who looked like they were high on drugs. One, a white guy, probably around 25 years old, was curled in a fetal position on the floor in the corner of the room. He was mumbling and visibly shaking. It looked like white foam was coming from his mouth, and his clothes were mussed and stunk bad.

She sighed and turned to me. "My manners. I haven't even asked your name."

"Emilio," I said, and it came out like a croak. I cleared my throat and repeated, "Emilio."

After sitting there for over an hour, I could tell she was becoming impatient especially when she said, "It's going to be a while before we even see the check-in nurse."

I took a look at the long line. "Feels like forever," I said. "Hopefully it will go fast."

By then, Pedro had stopped tearing, but his hand was turning a deeper blue-and-purple, and his skin was looking blotchy. I was guessing he had at least two or three broken bones. All I kept thinking about was the story he told me about when his father died and how he'd gone to the hospital to identify him. I wondered if we were at the same hospital, and if so, how being there was making him feel. I cringed when I pictured a doctor uncover his father and Pedro seeing the face. He was a young kid with a tough life, and now an injured hand would only set him back further.

I needed to stop thinking about Pedro. But I was wondering how long he'd stayed in school, whether he could read and write. And I promised myself that, if I stayed in Phoenix, I would teach him.

I sat there restlessly, wondering why the woman had stayed with us. She could have dropped us off and gone on her way. She owed us nothing. All I could figure was that Pedro was young and she felt she was doing the right thing.

We had been there another hour when Sara said to Pedro, "Look, I'm going down the block to get coffee. I'll be back soon." She turned to me. "Interested?" I wanted to blurt out *yes* because

I really wanted to go with her, but I knew my loyalty was to Pedro. "I'll stay with Pedro," I said.

He smirked. "I'm a big boy.  Go ahead."

CHAPTER 4

THE SUN HAD GONE down and it was raining when Sara and I left the Emergency Room. We made our way to her car, where she opened the trunk and took out an oversized black umbrella. We left the car and began strolling down the street. A block and a half down East Fillmore, we entered at a busy café on the ground level of an office building.

We sat by a window facing the boulevard. The tables were filled with people chatting and sipping coffee, a belt-driven ceiling fan spinning slowly above. Sawdust covered the floor—marketing throwback to former times. I was amazed how meeting Pedro on the street had led to me sitting there with a beautiful white American gringa.

She wasn't saying much. "So, you come here often?" I asked

lamely.

"Nah.  First time."

"Me, too," I said and laughed.

She signaled for a waitress.

In the far corner, close to the rest rooms, I spotted the back of a man wearing a Stetson hat with red hair spilling out of it, and my heart began to beat fast.  I could've sworn he was the same guy, but I shouted to myself, *Pull yourself together. What would he be doing in a place like this?*

"You look worried, my friend—Emilio you said your name was, huh?"

"Yes. . . ."

"Stop worrying.  Pedro will be okay when we get back.  It's probably just a simple fracture."

I wasn't about to explain my whole story to someone who would most likely be out of my life by the end of the day. The man with the Stetson rose from his stool.  I froze, but when he turned toward the door I could see he wasn't the same guy I had been picturing under the bridge and when I tramped through the  night in the desert, picturing his face and then, before I knew it, sworn I saw him hiding behind an outcrop or stalking me from behind a tree, startled every time I heard a noise.  When I laid my head down, he was on my mind, and when I awoke I thought I would find him standing over me.

I glanced at my watch.  "Pedro's probably still waiting."

But for some reason I kept staring at that man, even though he wasn't Arturo's murderer.

"So, Emilio," Sara said at last, "tell me about yourself."

We started talking, and soon the anxiety I felt sitting with such a bombshell went away, and I began feeling comfortable sitting with her. We talked about everything from school to my farming coffee and distributing it to hotels that catered to foreign tourists in San Salvador. She was well educated, fun, and beautiful, and—big news—I felt myself falling for her.

"Can I get you more coffee?" It was the waitress.

I looked at Sara. She smiled. "It's okay," she said.

"Just half a cup, please," I said to the waitress. Sara was having a croissant with butter and a cup of coffee. I had a chocolate chip muffin and a coffee.

I stared slyly at her eyes, thinking about her and me. What were the chances that maybe she was attracted to me the way I was to her?

"I can tell you're a good friend to Pedro. He's a nice boy."

"Yeah, he is. We're from the same country."

"Oh, yeah? That's a nice coincidence. Interesting that the two of you should meet. . . ."

We finished our coffee and strolled back to the hospital. When we entered the Emergency Room, a nurse told us that a doctor was seeing him. We took a seat.

The addict in the corner was still on the floor, shaking and rocking back and forth. "Do you think they can help him?" I said.

"They are. He got what he needs. It's raining, and he's sleeping in here, wasting away. That's enough help."

*Is it really?* I thought. *There has to be something else they could do for him. Maybe some pills to lessen the effects of the withdrawal? Maybe send him to a rehab? Or give him a meal?*

What shocked me most was Sara's attitude. She seemed to be looking down on him, and judging from the way she spoke, I didn't think she would have cared if the man had died right there on the floor. At that moment something about her made me think, or was I too consumed with her being larger than life? She *was* just a person, and we each had our opinions.

Then her attitude seemed to change. She was smiling at a baby rolling a toy car back and forth on the linoleum floor. "He's cute," she said.

Her company kept me from thinking about my mother and Arturo. I had been edgy since he was murdered, but, stranded there in Phoenix, I was starting to wonder about what I had to do next. I wanted to be home with my family, but I forced myself to put all those worries aside, to know more about Sara.

I was about to ask her a question or two about her life when Pedro came out of the swinging ER doors, smiling and waving his cast at us. "Two broken bones," he exclaimed somewhat proudly.

"I'm real sorry, Pedro," I said.

"No worries. You know, it's not paining like it was."

"Well, that's a good thing, honey," Sara said, wrapping her arm around him. She seemed to have a soft spot in her heart for him, like an older sister.

We were pulling out of the parking lot when Sara said, "It's late. You guys are welcome to stay at my place tonight." She paused.

"You can finish helping me tomorrow morning.  How's that?"

I said, "Of course I can.  And Pedro, don't worry.  I won't expect much from you.  I can do most of it myself."

CHAPTER **5**

**W**HEN WE GOT TO Sara's apartment, she made us each two hamburgers with big portions of broccoli and carrots. I realized that I had so abused my body with lack of food and rest that I was getting woozy, faint. "You got to eat the good food with the bad," she said, serving us at the dining room table. She added, "Everything in moderation, and keep your food balanced."

"Smells good," I said.

Pedro bent down over his hamburgers and took in a deep breath. "Smells delicious," he said.

We sank our teeth in. Her outlook on food made a lot of sense. I felt better and balanced after the meal.

Our next step was to take showers, then head off to bed. Pedro went first. I was sitting on the couch that had broken Pedro's hand when Sara came over and asked, "So what brought you to Phoenix?"

"Actually, I need to be in L.A."

"Cali?"

"Yeah. I have a friend who's going to take me across the country to New Jersey."

"How are you going to get to L.A.?"

I shrugged.

"Waiting on a coyote to get you there?" she asked, a smile playing across her face.

I guess she had picked up my sudden discomfort and laughed. She reached out and touched my arm. "Don't worry. Your secret is my secret. A handsome young man like you squeegeeing cars has to be someone in transition. I've seen a lot of you guys 'passing through?' That a good way to say it?"

"I guess," I said sheepishly.

"Suck it up, my friend. It's just life, and it happens to all of us." She shrugged.

"Thank you."

". . .If you want, I can take you there when I leave for San Fran."

"You would?"

She shrugged again. "Why not? You would definitely be good company." And she winked; I couldn't believe she'd winked at me.

It was an excellent idea. If she could drop me off in L.A. by the end of the week, I could arrange to have the coyote meet me and hitch a ride with another load of men. That should put me in New Jersey in a little over a week.

We sat there until we heard Pedro shut off the shower. "I got something for you to wear," Sara said, and got to her feet. "Come with me."

She took me into her bedroom.  It was gorgeous. The bed had eight beige pillows complementing her white comforter.  She had a vanity mirror with a picture of her and, I guessed, her girlfriends. A few stuffed teddy bears were sitting on the nightstand.  It was clean and felt comfortable.  She took me to a walk-in closet. There were a lot of men's clothes on hangers.  "My ex's stuff," she said. "And he'll be an ex a long time. You and Pedro can take whatever you want.  Pack as much stuff as you could in your backpack, because I'm leaving it all here."

"Okay!  Thank you, Miss Sara!"

"Leave that 'Miss Sara' for Pedro," she said.  "Call me Sara."

"Okay, Sara."

"For now, why don't you pick something both of you can wear?"

I found a black T shirt with a legend on the front that read *Cider's Pub* and, on the back, a big white *2*.  I grabbed two pairs of jeans, one for me and one for Pedro, and a blue T-shirt with a man on a surfboard riding a big wave that I thought Pedro would like.

"Thanks again," I said.

"Anytime.  Now, get out.  I need to get some rest," she said, smiling.

I found Pedro, wrapped in a towel in the living room, removing the plastic bag he had used to cover his cast.  His fine black hair was all over the place, and he smelled like soap.

"Here, put this on," I said, tossing him the clothes.

"Thanks, *mi amigo*."

"There's more where that came from."

"More clothes like this?"

I told him about the wardrobe; he beamed.

After I showered, I lay on the couch for a while. Pedro was already asleep in the recliner. He was a nice kid, and I was glad that we'd met and even thought about staying in Phoenix to help him when I realized I had to do what was best for my mother, that I would have to make my way to L.A. as fast as I could.

In the morning, I woke up before Pedro and found a pile of men's clothing on the sofa in Sara's living room. She must have brought it all out some time in the night. I'm glad that my backpack had some capacity.

I began packing as many tops as possible into my backpack. As I did, Pedro kept snoring with his mouth open, his injured hand resting innocently against his forehead. I saw a lot of myself in him. We'd both came to America to prosper and to help our families, both had our tragedies, but his were far worse. After all, I told myself, my father is alive, and I'm older and now more able. But Pedro had managed to survive on the streets, and I hoped he would be okay, that he would get a break in life and move ahead: He couldn't live a long healthy life in a makeshift home under a bridge.

For as long as I could remember, I had always enjoyed the morning, as if there was some kind of energy in the air that made me feel good. I stretched my arms and legs. The sun was peeking through the blinds, dust motes floating in the light air. I was starting to feel better.

All I had was time to kill, so I began moving the boxes she had stacked in the corner toward the front door. I gathered the dining room chairs and put them in the living room, close to the door. I was organizing all her stuff so it would be easy to take downstairs. I put boxes of similar size together and left the odd-sized smaller ones to the side. It would be easier to put the bigger ones on the bottom of the dolly.

Sara must have heard me working because she came out of her bedroom, rubbing her eyes. "Hey, baby, you're up early."

"I'm not the type who needs a lot of sleep," I said.

She pointed to Pedro. "Let him rest. The pain killers must have sent him to another planet."

Judging from the deep sleep he was in, I had to agree. I kept hauling her stuff past him, and he didn't even move. He was asleep *that* deep.

Sara tossed me the keys to the U-Haul truck and helped me load as many boxes as we could onto the dolly and pushed it downstairs. Once at the truck, she helped me organize it neatly so her things could fit without damaging anything. Within three hours, we had most of her furniture out of the door, except her bed, the couch and the recliner Pedro was sleeping in. The truck was just about full.

"Thanks for the help, Sara," I said. "For a woman, you're no slouch. You can work like a man."

She laughed as we got back upstairs. She was growing fast on me.

"I'm going to take a shower," she said.

"I'll keep packing the rest of the stuff…"

By the time I was finishing in the apartment, Sara had showered and dressed and was leaning against the green granite-topped island in the kitchen. She called out, "Come and have some coffee."

I wiped the sweat from my brow and went in the kitchen. She was munching granola. I had donuts with my coffee. Leaning there in tight jeans and a black belly top that read *Baby Girl*, she had a natural beauty, and I could hardly detect any make-up. Her hair was almost dry from the shower, and she smelled clean— and sexy. Something about her made me want to smile.

I was sipping my coffee and munching on the donuts when she said, "You're an okay kind of guy, you know, handsome. . . ."

"Oh. . .thanks," I said, embarrassed. It felt good to hear it from such an attractive woman. I guess a shower the night before and a fresh set of clothes had made a difference. I no longer had that filmy feeling across my skin. My hair felt light and fluffy. And the shower had brightened my mood.

By then, Pedro had awakened. He came into the kitchen and stood there with us. "Here, baby, this is for you," Sara said, handing him a breakfast bar and a cup of coffee.

"Ah, thank you, Miss Sara."

"Don't worry about helping. Emilio already did most of the work."

He looked at me and was nodding when he said, "I see. *Muy rapido.*"

After breakfast, I finished packing the U-haul. I was done by noon.

I was standing in the living room when Sara came in and handed us each thirty dollars. Pedro put the money in his pocket and started for the door. "*Gracias*, Miss Sara," he called out. "You coming with me, Emilio?"

"Yes, I'm coming."

"Emilio," she said, "don't forget that I'll be giving you a lift to L.A., okay?"

Pedro's face lit up. "Hey, Emilio, that's good for you!"

I turned to her. "Is there anything else you want me to help you with before we leave?"

"There might be, you know," she said thoughtfully.

I turned to Pedro. "You know what, Pedro? I'll catch up with you, okay?"

"Okay," Pedro said. "You know where you can find me at the end of the day."

"I know," I said grinning.

He nodded and waved his cast. "*Adios,*" he said, humped his enlarged backpack, and was soon out the door.

We spent the rest of the afternoon walking around the city and strolling through the park. She said she didn't have anywhere to be, and that she would miss Phoenix when she left in three days. Pedro was about all I would miss. I would remember him and Sara the most. And I would never forget the lessons I had learned on the street.

After leaving the park we stopped at a deli and had a tuna fish sandwich on a hard roll.  It tasted delicious, and Sara reminded me, "It's healthy."

I was starting to really get into her eating thing.  I felt the better nutrition was helping my body get stronger.  I had beaten the heck out of it crossing the desert.  The food helped to calm my anxiety.  With a full stomach, I was able to think clearer and deeper.

The rest of the afternoon was wonderful—and it gave me a chance to spend some time alone with her.

CHAPTER **6**

 IT WAS LATE WHEN we got back to her apartment. When we walked in, a man was sitting on her couch. The look he gave me was weird, and he was sitting as if he'd been counting the minutes, like a parent waiting for a child to return home past curfew.

"Hey, Dustin," Sara said, tossing her purse next to him.

"Hey, baby," he said coldly, looking at me. "Where were you? And who the hell is *this?*"

"Well, didn't you notice all of the stuff is out?  He did it."

"I could give a shit," the guy snapped, got to his feet, and strode over.  "Just why—why are you wearing my shirt? . . . Are those my *jeans?*"

The shirt fit loosely, and I'd had to roll up the hems. "Um," I said.

Sara stepped between us, pushed him away from me and

snapped, "Obviously, jerk.  But when he was doing the job *you* should've done, he slipped in the garage.  Grease ruined his. What's the big deal?"

"I'll tell you what the big deal is, Sara. You're screwing this up. Julio's on his way over, and you're playing caregiver. You're at odds with yourself.  So send this wetback on his way!"

I started for the door. "Thanks for the job and the food," I said, my voice almost a whisper.

Sara snapped, "Hey, get back here!  Don't you listen to this asshole!  Didn't I promise to take you to L.A.? You can stay."

"Bullshit, Sara!"  It was Dustin.

"No, no. You need to shut the hell *up*.  If Julio's coming tonight, we're leaving tomorrow.  And he's coming *with* us!"

I was caught in the middle of their argument.  "Should I just leave?" I asked.

"No, Emilio!"

The guy shrugged. "You got to be kidding me. We have *business* to transact with Julio. You *remember* our business, don't you?"  He sighed, "Your new—" he looked scornfully at me— "plaything– helper–whatever cannot *be* here.  And there's no *way* he's driving with us!"

Sara stared at him for a moment. "You see, you're wrong again. Whose car are we taking?"

He fell silent, looked angry.

"That's right!" she said.  "It's my car, so *I'll* decide who rides in it! You. . .well, now you're out. You're going to have to ride in the U-haul with that driver we hired."

Dustin let out a breath of what I interpreted as disgust, rolled his eyes, and crossed his arms. "Like *hell* I'm riding in that U-haul." He paused. "You *know* we don't need him here."

". . .What's the big deal, Dustin? He can stay in the dining room when Julio comes over."

"Yeah, whatever," he said, not keen on the idea, and turned to me again with a threatening look on his face.

He was much taller than me, well over six feet, and his eyes were hard and cold. In some indefinable way he reminded me of Arturo's murderer: I sensed the violence in him, and I was prepared to steer clear. "I don't want any trouble with you," I said.

"Trouble? You stay here, and you're going to have more than just trouble," he said.

I was scared and confused. I didn't understand what was making this guy so angry. Must be her boyfriend, I thought. But he didn't look like the type she'd date. He had a combed-over hairstyle where the ends of his brown hair on the right side of his face touched the front of his thick, black-rimmed glasses. He seemed in his mid-thirties, skinny, with narrow shoulders and hands too big for his body.

But who was I to judge? I didn't look as if I belonged with her either. Love was a powerful thing, I was thinking, and if he *was* her boyfriend, it had overlooked a lot.

He said, "Maybe you should just leave. Do yourself the favor."

"No, he's staying!" she said with an air of finality, grabbed my arm, and led me to the dining room. We locked eyes. "You stay in here," she said. "I'm sick of his shit. Everything will be okay. Get yourself a snack or something."

Before I could say a word, she had turned back. I could see what was going on.

"I've decided," I heard her say to Dustin, "not to go along with this Julio thing. I'm getting out of it."

"Oh, no, baby," he said, shaking his head, incredulous. "It's too late for that. Julio's coming with the money. He expects the deal we gave him. Forget about getting out."

A heavy knock on the door interrupted them. And then I heard the sound of someone impatiently fiddling with the lock.

"Speak of the devil," Dustin muttered, got off the couch, and opened the door. A large Mexican man pushed his way into the apartment.

"Hello, Julio," Sara said.

The man was a brute with a ragged scar on his face that looked like a knife wound. His biceps looked like cantaloupes under his short-sleeved shirt. The peaks of his traps nearly touched his ears, making it seem as if he had no neck. His face, and his jerky movements, suggested that he was not in much of a mood and not the type you messed with. He tossed a brown briefcase onto the couch. "Here's the money. Where's the stuff," he said gruffly, in a deep voice.

"We don't have it," Sara said, standing firmly before him.

"It's in her room somewhere," Dustin said flippantly.

"I *said* we don't *have* it!" Sara snapped.

Julio was shaking his head. "You couldn't be messing with me, senorita," he said, and turned to Dustin. "You know where it is?"

Dustin got to his feet and started for her bedroom.

At that moment, I knocked over a glass with my elbow. It shattered on the tiled floor of the dining room, and the big man whirled, a black handgun drawn.

"Who the hell is in there?" he demanded. "You guys setting me up or something? *Estupido pendejos.* I'll kill the both of you!" He crept into the dining room, and saw me.

"Who the hell are *you?*" he shouted, his weapon leveled at my chest.

"Don't mind him," Dustin said, emerging from the bedroom with an aluminum case. "He's Sara's new foster child or something."

The big Mexican grabbed me by my collar and dragged me into the other room so effortlessly I could've been a rag doll. I landed on the couch next to the brown briefcase.

"Yes. Where were we?" Julio asked, as if I were of no consequence.

"Here's what you bought, *amigo*," Dustin said, handing the aluminum case to him.

Julio reached for it, but Sara lunged and grabbed for it too. Dustin slapped her hard across the cheek, and she fell to the floor.

Oh, shit. I felt as impotent as wallpaper. Julio grabbed the aluminum case and nodded to the briefcase on the couch. "I've paid you two well, haven't I? What, someone suddenly having doubts? Huh, *amigos?*" His laugh sounded as if it was coming out of a wooden barrel. He pointed to the case. "I'm no chemist. You better be there to finish the job." He was speaking to Sara.

"Yes," said Sara, holding her cheek.

Julio nodded to Dustin. "You, too."

"You can guarantee it," Dustin said.

Julio said, "If not, I'll track both of you down and kill you." He said flatly and nodded, his face set cold. "You know, I have eyes and ears all around. Mess with me and this stuff, and I'll find both of you, and I will personally *kill* you. That's no idle threat, *chicas*. If you're not there to finish the job, you're as good as dead." He turned to the door.

"No worries, big man," Dustin assured him. "We'll keep our part of it. I can guarantee that."

Julio stopped and hovered above me. "So you're a witness, huh?"

I said nothing. I was too scared to talk.

"Do you know what witnesses get? . . . Stand *up* when I'm talking to you, you sonofabitch!"

I rose, and before I could see it coming he had thrown a jab so hard to the right side of my jaw, I could've sworn he'd cracked a molar. I grabbed the couch for support. Without it, I'd have hit the floor. Julio continued to punch me down into the couch. I fell over the back and, within seconds, he was straddling me, punching my head into the floor. I tried to protect my face. I tasted blood in my mouth. It felt as if I had been hit by a boulder. His fist was like steel, and I was sure I could hear Dustin's laughter and Sara screaming at Julio to stop.

And then it was over. He paused over me. He wasn't even breathing hard. He said, "You don't belong in America. You should have stayed in your country and fought your government for a better life. Coward bitch, looking for the easy way. All you punks are the same." He spat in my face and turned for the door. I heard it slam.

"You okay, baby?" It was Sara's voice, and it was coming from far away.

I felt her arms around me, helping me to stand. "I'm okay," I said.

"No, you're not! Let me help you to my bedroom."

I sat on the corner of her bed, she went back, and the yelling began.

I heard Dustin shout, "You're not *thinking*, Sara! Do you think he won't torture your ass? Do you think you'll take me down with you? Hell, no! Do you know how much money's in this briefcase? Do you think you or I can spend *any* of it if we're dead?"

She snapped, "Fine! Just shut the hell up. You bastard, you make me sick!"

He sighed. "I just don't *know* about you any more! You've left me no alternative, Sara. I'm sorry, but I—"

A gunshot rang out. It sounded like a bomb had gone off. He let out a grunt, and I heard a thud. My heart stopped. I grew cold.

I came out to see what had happened. Smoke was floating heavily in the room. It tasted sweet and filmy. I saw Dustin on the floor, gripping a bleeding knee. Next to him was an angular automatic pistol. Sara was standing above him with a small .32-caliber handgun. She stepped up to him and kicked away the automatic. It clunked against the wall near where I was standing. "So," she said, sneering, "what were you going to do? Kill me? Huh?" She looked up and saw me.

"Don't shoot," I stammered.

"Put your hands down, Emilio!" she snapped. "You've got to help me. Now there'll be danger waiting in every shadow for me!"

"H-how will *I* be able to help you?"

I stood there as if my sneakers had been stitched to the rug. What'd happened to the lovely Sara from earlier? Why had *this* happened? And why did she have a weapon, and the capacity to use it? I didn't know about women like this; I thought you only saw them in the movies.

Dustin was still rolling around on the living room carpet, squinting and shouting, "My *God*, my *leg!* You *knee- capped* me, bitch! Screw you!

"I think you're the one who's screwed right now, Dustin."

He grunted, "You think you'll get *away* with this?"

"You ought to drag your pitiful self to the bathroom and tend to that leg," she said to him, and turned to me. "We've got to go. You with me?"

"Y-yes." I stammered.

"Okay, first, pick up his gun, and then give me a hand!" she said, snapping a finger toward her bedroom.

I retrieved the weapon and handed it to her with trembling hands. She took it and marched off. I followed her.

She pointed to a black suitcase in the corner. "Grab that, and let's go!"

I did what she said and, on the way out, found my backpack on the couch. Dustin's blood was staining the carpet. She grabbed the briefcase full of money that Julio had left on the couch.

By this time, Dustin had dragged himself to the bathroom. "Emilio, we've got to go!" she said. "Somebody had to've called the police by now." She opened the door and peeked into the hallway. "It's clear. Let's do it!"

It was easy carrying her luggage to the elevator because I was amped up with adrenaline despite the beating I'd taken—I could have lifted a house. But I was scared too and uncertain of what I had gotten myself into.

Then it hit me. I was a *witness*. She needed me to keep my mouth shut—but what about Dustin? In time someone might find him. He could even call the cops himself. And when he eventually made it to a hospital, wouldn't they be asking questions?

But maybe whatever had been in that aluminum case Julio took away, whatever kind of business it was, had just gone down bad. That was not good! And I didn't think a guy like Dustin, would involve the cops. It would only expose him. Or was I completely wrong?

We reached the lower level, where she parked her car.

"Can you drive?" she asked me.

"Yes."

"Then drive."

I wasn't sure why she wanted me to, but when I got in and she stuck that dainty little handgun in my ribs, I completely understood. "Now if you try something stupid like change your mind and try to run away, I'll pull the trigger," she said.

"I won't, I promise."

It made sense. With me driving, she had total control over me. There was no way to jump out at a traffic light or stop sign. I did what she said and pulled out of the building. I was terrified, and all I could think about was an escape plan that wouldn't get me shot.

CHAPTER **7**

I KNEW THAT, IF I did what I was told, everything would be okay. If Sara told me to speed up, if she told me to turn left or turn right, I did.

Rain clouds had again darkened the Arizona sky. Then it began to pour. The thumping wipers could hardly keep up with the deluge on the windshield. We made a few turns through the city until she directed me to an entrance to Route 93 North. I had my hands glued to the steering wheel, going as fast as she said, swerving in and out of the dim red taillights ahead. My headlamps were barely visible on the roadway. I had no idea whether I had cut off a police car, hoped I had—my only chance of escape would be if a cop pulled us over. But who knew? She might have shot the cop.

There had been few words to describe the possessed look on her face when she shot Dustin. She'd seemed angry and delighted at the same time.

"Go faster, Emilio!"

"Okay, okay!" I realized my grip on the steering wheel was getting so tight I could have snapped it straight off the column. I wasn't sure where I was or where we were headed—somewhere in Arizona, and I needed to be in L.A..

If only Poppa knew what was happening to me.

When I got on the freeway, there were flooded stretches. Waves of rainwater were arcing away from fenders. I knew it was dangerous, but had I slowed down, I risked stalling the engine, so I kept even pressure on the pedal. The steering wheel started to feel loose, as if I was steering a boat. The tires were losing contact with the ground. I was aquaplaning. I didn't want to take the chance of pissing Sara off, though, and I wasn't sure what a stalled car meant for me. Would she shoot me on the side of the road?

Sara was staring straight ahead through the rain-smeared window. "Where are you taking me?" I asked.

"Just drive the car, Emilio," she said tiredly. By then she had taken her dainty little pistol out of my ribs and laid it on her lap. "Stop being afraid of me. You're safe. I'm not a killer. Dustin's alive, isn't he?"

I breathed a monumental sigh of relief. She was looking out the passenger window, thinking deeply. Of what? She finally said with a sneer, "I *should've* killed the bastard!"

I had no idea what to say. I had no experience with women like this.

"Dustin's a scumbag!" she said. "Listen, you wanted to go to

L.A., right?"

"Yes."

"I'll drop you off in L.A., but until then you'd better stick with me. I'm sure that Dustin will call for help and find some way to get in touch with Julio." She sighed. "You may be able to help me—you know, two heads better than one?" She looked directly at me. "Can you shoot a gun?"

I swallowed. Arturo and I had found a gun once back in El Salvador and made up our own shooting range down by a waterfall that masked the sound of our gunshots. I hadn't turned out to be a marksman, but I'd been better than Arturo. When we finished with it, we had thrown it into the water.

"Yes," I heard myself say, "I can shoot a gun." I took a deep breath. "I-I don't know if I can shoot a *person*, though."

"Do you think you'd be able to shoot someone who was going to shoot you?"

I shrugged. "I guess. . . ."

"Good enough. I can assure you that people will soon be shooting at us."

I swallowed again.

We drove through the night. The sun came rising free of clouds, hinting at a beautiful day. At last, we pulled up at Kingman Airport. "Follow the signs for parking," Sara said.

I wove through the concourse and found the parking area.

"Good. We'll leave the car here," she said, pointing to an open parking spot.

I followed orders.

"Are we going to board a *plane?*" I asked.  I had no ID.  I was certain I would be turned away.

"Just trust me," she said.

We never went inside the airport.  Instead, she found a cabbie leaning against his vehicle outside the Arrivals door.  She tapped her knuckles along the driver's side front corner panel.  "Can you take a fare?" she politely asked.

The fifty-something cabbie, with his Kangol hat and collared yellow shirt, turned to us with a coffee mug and breakfast cake in hand.  "You *can* see I'm on break, huh?" he said.

"Sweetie, I just need to get to the closest car rental.  It won't take long—I'll make it worth your while."  She laid a folded bill in his hand.  I couldn't tell if it was a ten, a twenty, or a fifty.

"Break's over," the cabbie said.  "Hop in."

Sitting in the cab, I stole a glance at her.  God, she was beautiful.  I thought of Mata Hari.  Yet there was something about her that made me feel alive, and it wasn't just sexual.  I remembered how caring she had been when Pedro was hurt.  So though Sara was tough as a proverbial nail, there was a gentle side of her.  She had a strength I wished I had myself.  I thought of Arturo.  What had I ever done but whine and run away?

"What's with you, Emilio?" Sara said.

"Just thinking," I said.

I didn't want to think anymore of the coward I was, so I forced myself to think about Sara and why she wanted me to stay with her.  In a way I felt like a man.  She *had* said that she wanted my help against some bad guys.

The cab stopped on the western end of Kingman. The Alamo Rental had a sign that read *Serving West Kingman and All of Northwestern Arizona*.

We went inside and rented a red Chevrolet Cobalt with a sunroof.

"I'm sure this is not the first time you're renting a car," the young, pimpled, college-age clerk said as he completed the paperwork.

"Yes, yes," Sara said impatiently. "I'll make sure it's returned with the gas tank full."

"Okay," he said, grinning. "And it has to be back by noon."

"No problem," she mumbled.

Soon I was tailing her to the door.

When we got out and were standing on the sidewalk, waiting for the valet to deliver the Cobalt, there were a lot of people around.

I saw a homeless man walking across the street who reminded me of Pedro. Was he okay? That night I spent with him under the bridge, he'd told me the cops constantly pushed him around, that before he found a nest under the bridge, they had roused him from different squatting areas in the city. He had boasted about how well hidden his home was under the bridge. They hardly peeked around there.

The Cobalt was nothing like Sara's BMW—a lot slower, the seats stiff, the steering wheel tighter. It had a beige cloth interior, and the radio was mostly static. But who was I to complain? The best thing my father had back home was a 1988 Toyota pickup with body rot, a loud muffler, and bad shocks.

Sara pulled out a highlighted map from her purse, and began giving me directions. We headed back onto Route 93 North for what felt like a lifetime, stopping once for a quick bathroom break and snacks.

We drove along the orange-and-crimson mountains nestled under a big sky, not saying much. We both had our problems.

By then, the evening sun had long chased the moon. As we traveled through that barren terrain, I began to wonder if we were indeed heading to Los Angeles. But I didn't say anything. She was in charge. It was getting dark as we continued on Route 93 North.

At that moment, Sara surprised me by stroking a finger behind my ears, lightly rubbing the knotted muscles along the back of my neck. It shot a sense of strength and warmth straight through me. "You're a handsome guy," she whispered.

I couldn't help but smile. "Thanks," I said warily. Who was I but someone she met cleaning her windshield at a traffic light? ". . .Sara, can you maybe tell me what's going on? I mean, what is this all about, you know, Dustin and this Julio guy, the money, the stuff that Dustin gave him?"

"What I can tell you is that we got lucky back at my place, and I'm truly sorry I got you involved." She sighed. "I like you. I guess you won't be able to say the same about me—you know, holding a gun on you, forcing you to drive."

I shrugged. "Despite all of this, I'm still glad I met you. You're taking me to L.A. I'm thankful for that."

She offered a tepid smile before nibbling on my ear.  I felt goose bumps.

"I won't be able to concentrate on my driving if you do stuff like that, Sara."

"Okay, Mr. Driver," she said and laughed.

My heart was fluttering as I relaxed my shoulders, keeping my eyes on the road.  It was dark, and the evening breeze swept through the Cobalt. The tension left me.

The moon was bright and highlighted Sara's bunched-up dress, showing her long smooth legs.  It looked sexy.  But she spoiled my good thoughts when with a cold tone, she said, "He got what he had coming to him.  I hope he bled to death, that piece of shit!"

I sensed she was done with the romance.  She leaned back and closed her eyes.  "Just stay on this road."

CHAPTER **8**

ARRIVING IN LAS VEGAS is like landing a mammoth alien ship on Earth after a billion miles of nothing. . .a collection of strobe lights set in neon and glass, a glowing gem in the middle of the desert. The lights were flickering and sparkling so vibrantly on the hood of the Cobalt, it was as if we had pulled into a space station on Jupiter, a video game of light and energy and movement.

"Why are we here?" I asked.

"Believe it or not, I don't know.  I guess I always wanted to see what Las Vegas looks like before I die. . . ."

*Shit!*  I thought.  *Is she having a premonition of death?  Am I going to die, too?*

We had driven down Las Vegas Boulevard to the south end when, smiling like a kid in a candy store, she pointed out a strikingly massive illuminated green building with the letters *MGM* glowing in yellow lights on the top. The place looked like enormous sticks of kryptonite shining brightly. A crowd had gathered around a guy painting something with spray-cans on the sidewalk. It was night, but it seemed like the middle of the day. Throngs of people were moving along, some holding hands; most seemed happy. One couple had just gotten married: She was still wearing a bridal gown, down to the veil, the man a tuxedo with a corsage. Vegas was everything I had expected

"Pull over here. We have to find a motel," she said. "Someplace small and inconspicuous. Someplace where Julio or Dustin wouldn't think I'd be staying. . . ."

We found a neat little motel and took a room with one large bed. It was almost midnight, and I was exhausted. My body felt beaten after all I had gone through.

"I need a shower badly," Sara said as I sat on the edge of the bed, and before I knew it, she was naked; it was as if I wasn't there in the room with her. "I hope you're not the shy type," she said as she opened her handbag.

"You're. . .beautiful," I croaked.

She turned with Dustin's handgun—handle first—to me. "Keep this. Sleep with it under your pillow."

"Okay," I said, and took it, feeling as if there was something crawling inside my face. I was holding a gun. It looked like a Glock. I examined it. It *was* a Glock, black and lethal.

When I looked up, her rear end was disappearing into the little bathroom. Why hadn't I invited myself in with her? I thought.

And then I heard her singing. She was really *singing!* I couldn't believe it. Twenty minutes or so later, she was out, wrapped in a beige towel. "Let me have that suitcase, Emilio. I need fresh clothes."

I lifted the suitcase onto the bed for her and told her I was going to take a shower, too.

"Knock yourself out, cowboy, but keep that gun with you," she said, and allowed the towel about her to slip to the floor as she looked for something new to wear.

"While you're in there, I'll order some food for us," she called after me. "What do you want?"

"Food!"

She laughed.

When I came out of the shower, she was speaking to someone on the phone. I heard the name 'Kathy.' She looked a little worried but soon brightened when we heard a rap on the door and a female voice call out, "Room Service?"

Sara signaled me to get out of sight and started for the door. I slipped back into the bathroom with the weapon raised, as if in a movie, and scared to death.

She cautiously opened the door to find a Hispanic woman with long black hair in a bun at the back of her head, who pushed a food cart into the room. Sara tipped her; she curtseyed and left.

Sara popped the cork on the bottle of champagne that had come with the food and said, "Cheers!"

"Cheers," I said, raising my glass. When I tipped it toward my mouth, some of the wine spilled down my fingers and onto the carpet.

We began to eat.  I thought of my parents.  Back home, there was no champagne, no alcohol, barely enough food to stay alive.  We farmed coffee, and our trade was dying.  Poppa was worried another bad season would put us out of business.  We grew most of our table food, but when a tractor broke or Momma needed to see a doctor, we were cash strapped.

The alcohol had gone to her head.  She started hugging me and smiling uncontrollably.  "C'mon, Emilio!  Why the long face!  Let your hair down, man!  We're *safe* here!"

Afterward, we embraced closely like lovers do, and stumbled to the king-sized bed.

And fell asleep, too tired to do anything else.

CHAPTER 9

**F**OR THE FIRST TIME in two weeks, I woke up in a bed, and next to a beautiful woman. The air was stale. The sun was peeking through the drapes well before Sara considered peeling back the covers. A trail of clothes led from the door to the bed. The empty bottle of champagne had rolled under a chair.

I was still a bit groggy, but my mind was not. I was going to ask Sara what I had gotten myself into. I had a gun, and our lives were in danger. It was only right that I knew why I was going to die if it came to it. She couldn't deny it. Then I remembered the care she had taken to hide the briefcase that Julio had left—gone into the bathroom with it, and even though I went in after her, there was no sign of it.

I glanced at her. Stone asleep. I tiptoed to the bathroom and looked around. I looked in the little cupboard under the sink. I looked up—it had to be—and spotted a loose rectangle of ceiling tile. I climbed onto the toilet seat. Sure enough, I found the briefcase there and took it down. There was no combination lock, only a regular leather clasp that opened easily to reveal more money than I had ever seen in my life.

It seemed like a million dollars in cash.

I reached in with trembling fingers and took out a wad of it. "Oh, my God!" I whispered and put it back very quickly. Big money from a guy like Julio meant big trouble. I slipped back the wad, replaced the briefcase, and returned to the bedroom with a deep yearning to speak to my parents.

Sara was still snoring peacefully. As I got into some clothes, I couldn't help but consider whether I could love a woman like her, or she me—considering who she was, her associates, the money, and the danger we were in.

I took a deep breath. I needed to talk to my father. It might be the last thing I did. I'd hit the street and buy a phone card with some of the money from loading the U-Haul. Sure that my billfold was in my back pocket, I started for the door.

Then I remembered the automatic under my pillow. "No," I whispered to myself, "without her by my side, I'll just be another *amigo* on the street," and left the motel room.

I bought a phone card at a gift shop outside the MGM hotel and ambled down Las Vegas Boulevard. It was a dry, hot morning, and there were no signs it would cool off anytime soon. The sun was bright. A man pointed me in the direction of a payphone, only it was across the street, and a concrete median in the middle with a chain-linked fence fastened to the top forced me to take the long way. So I went to the corner, across the street and down the block before I found a payphone kiosk next to the Mandalay Bay monorail.

The plastic handle of the phone was warm. Anxious, afraid of the inevitable—I knew Momma needed me to hurry, to send money quickly—I was focused on doing my best, but my journey could end right where I was. If she had passed away, there was no point in me staying.

I dialed home with shaking fingers, letting out a deep breath. "Poppa, it's me. How's everything?"

"Emilio, bless the Lord. *Como estas?*"

"I'm okay," I lied.

"You in New Jersey?"

"Not yet, Poppa, I'm in Nevada."

"Nevada? *Porque?* Arturo's mommy called and told me that she found out that you and Arturo ran together after the van had a flat and the police was coming. I was worried for the two of you."

"I'm okay, Poppa. How's Momma?

"*Que no esta bueno.* She needs medicine. She was bad this morning, you know. We need to find money desperately, Emilio. I'm trying—I'm even trying to borrow." I heard my father's voice crack with the inability to take care of the woman he had loved for so many years. It chilled my blood. And I swore that I was *not* going to allow her to die while I was on the run with a woman who had a briefcase full of cash.

"Don't worry, Poppa, I'll wire you money soon—enough to make Momma good like new!"

"*Por favor*, my son," Poppa said, his tears flowing at last.

"Poppa, stop crying. I promise I won't let you down. Just let that coyote guy know his man with the van screwed up and that I'm still trying to get to New Jersey. Let him know that we're paying him a lot of money, and that he has to take care of the connections. Tell him I made it to Phoenix, and no one was waiting for me. I'm hitching a ride to L.A. and should be at the Union Terminal within a day or so! I'll call you to arrange a time to meet him. Tell him not to screw up again."

"Yes, I will remember, my son. How's Arturo?"

". . .We got separated, Poppa. I don't know where he is right now."

"If you see him, tell him to call his mother. She's worried sick."

"And, Poppa," I ended, "if in the end they tell you that I was not at the Union Terminal waiting to be picked up, don't worry. I'm here to help Momma, and that is what I will do. Okay?"

"Thank you, my son."

A loud bread delivery truck pulled up. I leaned into the kiosk. "I have to go now, Poppa!" I shouted. "I love you!"

"*Mi amor.* Be careful, Emilio."

The dial tone echoed through the wire. I pressed my forehead against the metal edge of the phone kiosk. It felt as if the sun had kicked out more beams directly at me, raising the temperature.

I turned away from the phone kiosk thinking about what Arturo and I had gone through, surprised my dad had heard about our detour so quickly.

This line of thinking got me wondering, and then it hit me. I needed to get to a computer and dig up some info about Arturo, at least to know what the red-bearded man had done with his body.

I found an internet café and had just enough money to spend twenty minutes online. I went right to it. I searched a national media site and turned up nothing. Ditto state and local news sites. So I tried different searches, like "burglar killed by Arizona home-owner," "Illegal immigrant caught and killed in Yuma County, Arizona," and "Arizona law permits homeowner to shoot intruder." I still came up with nothing involving Arturo. But on the last search, I found information that claimed Arizona permitted the killing of someone in defense of property. Right or wrong, I didn't like what I saw. That would mean I myself would be in a lot of trouble, and Arturo's death, as sick as it sounded, was justifiable homicide.

What I learned pissed me off, so I switched focus and hunted for information about Dustin getting shot or Pedro somehow hav-ing gotten involved—and there it was, an article headlined *Cleaning Gun, Man Accidentally Shoots Himself in Leg*, including a picture of him and of Arizona State Hospital. A police investigation had la-beled it an accidental self-inflicted wound. But this meant Sara wasn't wanted for a crime.

When I got back to the hotel room, she was sitting at the small round dining room table, legs crossed, smoking a cigarette. I still couldn't figure out why she ate healthy and smoked cigarettes. Housekeeping was in the hallway; the television was chattering something about the terror level being raised and the borders getting tighter. I heard the voice of a news anchor say something like, "Washington is ordering a massive dragnet to hunt terror cells."

Without looking up at me, she said, "Did you count how much is in the briefcase?"

I sat over from her. I looked her in the eye. "No, I didn't. How much money is?"

"Five hundred thousand. That is—"

"Half a million, Sara. I *can* count, you know. I'm not a dumb *wetback* as some of you call people like me!"

"Whoa! Take it easy, lover boy."

I got to my feet and began pacing. ". . .Look, you need to tell me what I've gotten myself into." I shrugged. "All I was hoping for was a lift to L.A., not this—a gun under my pillow and God knows what else."

"You're right," she said, stubbing her cigarette out in the cheap ashtray on the coffee table between us. "It's only fair that you know what's going on."

"And I really need some money, Sara. For my mother. . . she's very ill."

She sighed. "That's why you're here illegally, huh."

I nodded.

"I might not be able to help you with any of the money in the briefcase, Emilio, but I have a check for five hundred dollars that I can cash and let you have. . . . But first let me level with you about what's going on."

"I'd appreciate that," I said, feeling better. Maybe talking about my mother had caused it, maybe her promise of help.

"But first," she said, "Where did you go?"

"I called my parents—my father, actually."

"You wanted to find out about your mother," she said. "I understand. It's the same way I feel about my sister Kathy, and I'm praying that what I've gotten into will not affect her."

"Sara. . .what's going *on?*"

She leveled her eyes on me. "Listen. You remember the aluminum case that slime Julio took from my apartment?"

"Yes."

"What do you think it was?"

"Drugs."

"Shit, no. . . . It contained—it contained a canister of Sarin gas that. . .that I made." She took a deep breath. "I'm a chemist."

"What? Pedro said you own a restaurant."

She waved her hand dismissively. "I own that, too." She sighed. "That's why I got into this mess in the first place: to get the kind of money to open up a real classy restaurant in San Francisco."

"And who's Dustin? An old boyfriend?"

"He was. He's the one who hooked me up with Julio and his people." She shrugged.

I guess my brows furrowed as I glanced at her. "What's Sarin gas? What does it do?"

". . .Basically, it's to kill people, you know, chemical warfare?"

"So—*why?*" My eyes were starting to hurt. "W-why would you have something like that in your house?"

She said, "Julio used to be with the Frente Revolucionario. He's a fanatic, a—calls himself a 'revolutionary warrior'— blood hungry and hell-bent on killing people."

"You mean you made the gas for this Julio guy to *kill* people? What would the Frente gain from this? Who's it Julio wants to kill? *Americans?*"

"Yes."

"I don't understand. Why would the Frente want to kill innocent Americans? This isn't adding up."

"Listen, the Frente wanted *no* part of this. This is *Julio's* call. He's nuts. He's just nuts. He wanted to take over the Mexican government by killing all the government officials. I'm talking bombs, guns, fires, whatever. . . . Look, they *realized* he was too psychotic, too big of a liability, so they threw him out. The last time he was seen leaving Mexico, he said that, when he returned, the rest of them would owe him their lives, that *he* would be the one to bring them out of oppression through what he plans to do—and that through him, the whole world will know about their suffering. Generating global publicity, he says, is the only way to bring the cause of the Frente Revolutionario to the world."

"This is absolutely crazy. Terrorism is not what they're *about*, Sara!"

"So what *are* they about?" Her tone was sarcastic.

"*Shit.* . . . So what happened in your apartment?"

"I knew that Julio was coming to pick up the stuff." She shook her head.

"But you'd changed your mind."

"Yes."

"And why was Dustin so upset?"

"Well, the canister, and my notes on how to release the gas, were in that case. . . . It's more than just opening up a valve. That money in the briefcase was for the gas, the information, and Dustin and me setting it off. That's what he was afraid of—that I'd back out."

"But you shot Dustin so he couldn't do it, right?"

She shrugged again. "You never know with him."

"But—but if he can't do the job, Julio will have to find you to set it off. . . . Doesn't this mean that he can't kill you, since. . . ?"

She was silent.

I swore under my breath. "But first he'll have to find you—I mean us." I looked at her. "I guess by now he's found Dustin."

"Probably."

"Maybe they have already joined forces to find us," I said, feeling a chill in my belly.

"We've got to stay ahead of them."

"We'll be able to, Sara. This is a big country. It will be like looking for a needle in a haystack."

I wished she hadn't said what she said next. "I'm not so sure, Emilio. That's why from now on we always keep the guns handy." Then she got up. "I'll take a shower, and then we'll head out and find a joint that cashes checks."

"You think we should be seen together in broad daylight?"

"What do you suggest?" she said.

For a moment, all I could think of was how beautiful she was. "That we lie low and wait at least until tonight."

She settled back in the chair. "So," she said smiling, "what do you suggest we do for the rest of the day?"

"Get to know each other—what do you say?"

"We could do that." Her brow creased.

"What?"

"You're a quick thinker. Tell me some more about this Frente Revolutionario business that Julio represents."

"Well, actually, they're mostly known as a social movement based on an anti-globalization. They're opposed to the way the Mexican government runs things."

"Yeah, I know. Whatever. But you have to admit, they look a hell of a lot like al-Qaeda."

"Who cares what they *look* like? They put their guns down years ago."

"Yeah, yeah, peaceful protestors. Whatever."

I knew a lot about the Frente. Nearly everybody from my country did. They are a group of indigenous people who are distressed and upset with the Mexican government. They glorify Panco Villa and Emiliano Zapata. They have their own territory with a different set of rules, where the people are in charge and not the government.

She shrugged. "You had a shower yet?"

In my eagerness to call home, I hadn't taken a shower before I left.

"No."

"Would you like to wash my back?"

"*Would* I?" I said, laughing.

The stars began to dim across the dark Nevada sky like theatre lights softening before a show. We were going to first find a place to cash her check and then head out to California. A cool breeze swept through the Cobalt. The day had been good. Talk about getting to know Sara, it had been heavenly but hadn't lessened my worry over Julio even a little. And it was hard to accept her being part of a terrorist plot.

All I knew was that Julio had paid her to manufacture the gas, and even if she got away from him, there would still be Dustin, who maybe knew himself what to do with the stuff. And if she'd known that Julio's planned to murder Americans, why agree to do it in the first place? The thought that it was just for money made me squirm. I just could not think of a single reason to justify her involvement.

As if she had read my mind she said, "Julio is expecting a meeting with me in a week. I think he's planning to set the gas off soon."

"Damn! Where?"

"A subway in L.A."

"Holy shit!"

"So it will happen, if you say Dustin probably knows how to set it off."

"Probably. If he doesn't, they'll need to find me."

"Can they?"

"I don't want to think about it, Emilio." She pointed up ahead. "There! There's a place we can cash the check."

"What'd you say, Sara?"

"Aren't you listening to me?" she said.

"I think," I said, "that Mini Cooper has been following us."

She swiveled around, but the little black thing with tinted windows overtook us and disappeared around the corner beyond the check cashing store.

"False alarm," I mumbled apologetically.

C H A P T E R **10**

**T**HE STORE WINDOW WITH the orange neon light that read *Check Cashing, Low Rates* also featured signs for phone cards, cigarettes, and beer. A streetlight halfway down the block cast a flat, dim light on the front of the place. Some dirty rainwater had pooled close to the curb. The store seemed deserted.

We got out of the car with the briefcase inside a large shoulder bag Sara was carrying but left everything else in the back seat. I had the Glock in the oversized pocket of my beige cargo pants.

Sara went through her hand purse as I pressed a button on the lintel. When the buzzer went off and the door clicked, I pushed it open. There was a guy sitting like a bank teller behind a thick pane of glass with a hole the size of an orange through which you could speak.

"I have a check here," Sara said, but before she would go on the buzzer sounded again, and a blond, very bearded white guy with a bulbous nose hurried up behind us.

"Please," he said to Sara. "This is a a-cash emergency."

"Of course," she said, and stepped aside.

He whipped out a sawed-off shotgun and stuck it through the hole into the teller's face. "J-just touch that goddamn silent alarm below that desk, and you s-stop *breathing*!"

Another voice exploded from the door. "What the hell you doing again? We're not here to rob another bank! We're here for this bitch with the guy's money!"

"C-hill *out,* man!"

Sara and I turned at the same time and found ourselves staring into what looked like the barrel of a handheld bazooka in the hands of a tall, broad-shouldered man with a black ski mask.

The blond man said, "I'm an uh-entrepreneur, J-jack. D-deal with Julio's business while I make me a little extra pay here." He turned back to the teller, who was standing frozen with the shotgun in his terrified face. "Let me in behind there, or y-you're a dead mother!"

A buzzer sounded promptly, and a door opened in a wall off to the side of the encased counter. "T-that's what I'm talking about!" the blond guy said and disappeared into the inner room.

With my heart thumping like hell, the masked man signaled to Sara and me. "Out!"

Sara said, "Who—who are you? This is a big—"

"You have money you shouldn't have, Sara. . .for services you have not performed," he said, and laughed.

"Listen," she said, voice trembling as she reached into the hand purse, "you're mistaken. You've got the wrong person. I can show you my I.D.—"

Her hand came out firing. One round caught the guy in his left shoulder and his eyes flared in surprise. He had just gasped, "What the—" when she shot him twice more. He hit the ground, and she kicked away his weapon.

The blond guy came rushing out with a canvas bag in one hand and his shotgun in the other.

Sara screamed, "*Shoot* him, Emilio! *Shoot him!*"

I hesitated a second and saw the muzzle of the shotgun rise in my direction, and for an instant I could feel the blast hit my chest and the life drain out of me before Sara fired twice more in rapid succession, and he dropped the bag and reached uncomprehendingly for his bleeding stomach and began to sink to the floor. Sara seized me and pushed me towards the door. "Run!"

My ears were ringing still from the sound of her gun going off five times in a small room, and I realized I hadn't even pulled the automatic from my pocket. But there was the guy in the mask, grimacing in pain in the middle of the floor between me and the door.

I don't know what came over me, but I kicked him brutally in the head, and tripped.

"Let's *go!*" she said. She caught up with me at the door, in her hand the canvas bag the blonde had been holding. She tossed it to me. "Teller's tripped the alarm by now! *Out!*"

As we reached the door, I froze. A uniformed policeman, young and in combat stance, was pointing his weapon at us, behind him an idling LVPD patrol car. *"Freeze!* Get down on the ground!"

*"Now!"* another voice barked off to our left. He was an older cop with .44 magnum trained on us in a two-handed stance, his arms braced on the hood of the car.

I was in front, the weapon still in my pocket, masking Sara with the pistol in her hands. They were looking at me.

"Put your hands up!" the older cop shouted, his face a snarl.

I was doing so, still holding the bag, when she pushed me forward and fired.

*"No!"* I screamed to Sara.

As the older cop was diving down behind the car, the younger one fell back against the passenger door and started sliding to the ground.

We ran as fast as we could, past a black Mini Cooper.

By then the older cop was screaming on his police radio, "Officer down! Officer down!"

The sounds of more gunfire had pounded my eardrums, and a ringing, piercing sensation was driving me mad. I spun quickly, looking for the red Cobalt, but Sara was already shoving me hard in the back. "Move! Get *in!*"

We literally threw ourselves into the car. I landed in the driver's seat, and by the time I was shifting the Cobalt into drive, Sara had dived into the back, lying across the seats, shouting, "Keep your head low!"

I hammered the gas and sped off, spinning the wheel around the corner.

In the distance I heard the wail of sirens.

I had just seen Sara shoot another person for the fourth time within days. *Shit!* I swore to myself. Did she have to shoot the cop? Was he *dead?* But then. . . *If I end up in jail,* I told myself, *my mother's finished.*

I kept the gas pedal on the floor.

CHAPTER 11

**W**ITHIN MINUTES, WE WERE heading out of the city. I watched the buildings in the rear-view mirror get smaller, as if they were sinking into the earth. By then, the desert had cooled, and thick clouds were moving quickly above us. The traffic was light. I drove only a few miles over the speed limit. Finally, after all the commotion, silence overcame us. It gave me a chance to calm down, but it wasn't easy. I kept convincing myself the cop would live.

Breaking the silence, I said, "You didn't have to shoot the cop."

With a sneer, she said, "Oh? What *should* I have done?" I glanced in the mirror again to find her gesturing at me. "Oh, *I* see. It would've been better if we got caught. And I guess I should've let that stuttering imbecile put a bullet in you, too?"

I said nothing.

I hadn't forgotten how I'd behaved.  Actually, it was all I could think about—face-to-face with death, a shotgun being elevated to my chest, and I'd frozen.  If it hadn't been for her, I'd have died.  I exhaled onto the windshield, shaking my head.

She extended her arms between the seats and rubbed my shoulder.  "You don't have to be so hard on yourself.  I got you."

"I know.  Thanks.  I'm sure he'd've killed me."

She began to deeply massage my shoulder.  My muscles were still taut.  She murmured, "You're not the only person to be a little gun shy."

"It's not that, Sara.  I'm just a damn coward!"

"No, you're not. . . . As for me and guns, they're like a part of me.  I grew up with them.  Heck, nearly everybody from back home is handy with a pistol.  Daddy taught me.  I've hunted with him for years."  Her eyes widened.  "Yeah, Daddy taught me," she repeated.

"But I've shot a gun before, Sara."

"Have you?"  She stared out the window into the dark desert sky.  "I guess you shot beer bottles and things like that.  But have you ever shot a living thing?"

"No."

"That's the difference.  Me, I could hit a scurrying rabbit at a hundred yards, a deer at double that."  She said it with disappointment in her voice.  I could tell she was thinking, perhaps reminiscing, deeply.

She shook her head.  "Anyway, let's see what we got."

She opened the canvas bag and laid the bundles of cash, each individually wrapped and labeled *One Thousand*, on the seat.

"Ninety, Emilio. There's ninety thousand," she said, a smile nearly touching both ears. "We'll split it."

Thinking of my mother, I said, "Perfect. It's more than I need."

She took my half, stuffed it into a deep inner pocket of my back-pack, and zipped it up.

"You know what?" I said. "I need some of that money *on* me. You never know what can happen."

"True," she said, and transferred some of her share into my pocket.

With my eyes on the road, I said, "How much is it?"

"Two thousand," she said, laughing. "Pocket change."

"Pocket change," I echoed, smiling. "That's good."

She was repacking her half into the canvas bag when she shouted, "Wait! How'd they know we were in Vegas?"

She spun around, staring out the rear window. ". . .Dustin didn't know about Vegas."

"Why wouldn't he?"

"How could I tell him? What would I have said, that I was going to do something on a whim, like head to Vegas? Come on, Emilio, I didn't even know that myself."

It made sense. Somehow they had known. Had they been fol-lowing us the whole time? Or was it something else?

I started to feel warm, so I rolled down the window and a cool breeze swept through the Cobalt. The wind got me thinking. "Maybe there's a tracking device, something like that."

"What?"

I shouted over the wind and the growl of the engine, "A *tracking device!* Check the briefcase!"

Sara shouted, "Okay, roll up the *window*. I don't want bills all over the highway!"

I did, and she began to frantically rifle through the wads of cash. "Take your time," I told her.

She looked up from the briefcase and, in an exaggerated fashion, as if she was moving in slow motion, laid the bundles of cash neatly on the seat next to her, mortaring them tight, like bricks. "Is this slow enough?"

I glanced back at the pile of money. It looked even larger out on the seat next to her. I turned my eyes back to the road, and kept shifting to the rear-view mirror.

She turned the briefcase upside down and shook it. "Nothing," she said.

I said, "It's got to be some small electronic thing. Feel the case all over. Maybe it's in the walls."

She rubbed her fingers silently across the black velvet interior, along the edges, and toward the middle.

I had begun to whistle tonelessly when she shouted, "I feel something—yes!"

"You have some kind of blade? Cut it open and see what you find."

She fished a penknife from her handbag and soon had something between her thumb and index finger: an electronic device the size of a watch battery. She examined it like a jeweler appraising a diamond. It had a red LED the size of a pencil eraser blinking on the face of it.

"Shit, Emilio!  Roll down the window."

I did, and she tossed it out into the desert, leaned forward, her lips against my ear, and murmured, "Baby, thank you."

I set the cruise control and began to relax.  All I had to do now was monitor vehicles approaching from behind.  When the head-lights stayed in the mirror for too long, I switched lanes, slowed down and let them overtake us.  It seemed as if every car was fol-lowing us.

"Pull over up ahead," she said.  "At that lookout point.  I'm going to move up front."

I found a sweeping panoramic view when we got there; the peaks of distant mountains were barely visible across the dark sky.  I got out and stretched my arms and legs.  I stood against the edge of a railing and looked down to find a gushing river flowing heavily down the base of the valley. The tranquil sound of that water splash-ing against large rocks, and the sight of light glinting sporadically across the horizon, filled my senses.

We were soon back on the highway heading into the rising sun.  I was wide awake, my mind too active for sleep.  The smoke from Sara's cigarette lay heavy in the Cobalt.

I knew she had divided half the stolen money, and that made me a thief.  I wondered what the guy in the check-cashing store had said to the police.  Had we been caught on the security camera? And the two who had assaulted us—were they involved in the Sarin gas thing?

Sara stubbed out her cigarette in the ashtray in the center console and turned to me, I guess feeling self-conscious. Her voice, her whole demeanor, soft now, she said, "I know you think I've been a greedy bitch to have gotten myself involved with Julio in the first place, but I've got obligations."

"Obligations? What kind of obligations?"

"Money obligations. Family obligations."

"Sara, we all have obligations. The most important thing right now is us staying alive. And stopping this thing if we can. We've *got* to try, or plenty of people are going to die. No amount of money can justify something like that."

"Yeah, but Julio isn't going to back down. With or without a tracking device, his men are after us. God, you saw them—a bazooka and a sawed-off shotgun. I'm afraid if I don't help Julio, I *will* no doubt get killed." She shrugged. "To save myself, I don't have a choice."

"You can't be serious."

"*Enough*, Emilio. You think everybody thinks rationally. I'm not going to *die* over this. I can't. My sister. . . . Enough about this."

She turned on the radio. Soft jazz filled the interior. We continued toward L.A. I wondered if that was a good thing.

"But do you *really* think you're going to go through with it?" I asked abruptly.

"I'm just not sure what to do. This has spun way out of control." She'd said it calmly, not even with a crack in her voice. I saw something deep and dark. Her face cold, she said, "I think you think too damn much. Stop asking questions."

But my mind was racing. I was picturing the dead laid out in a makeshift mortuary and the national—international news coverage. I was imagining the tearful talking heads—the wives of husbands who'd died, the mothers of children who'd died: commuters, workers, kids going to school. I wondered if I should pull over and find the nearest police station.

CHAPTER **12**

**B**UT I DIDN'T PULL over—not because I wasn't sure it was the right thing to do, but because I wasn't ready to go to prison. Not to mention that, if the cop had died in Vegas, I'd be charged with murder along with Sara, and they threw away the key when it came to cop killers.

So although I hadn't decided anything, I gave Sara the impression I was going along with her. She was holding all the cards and had given me a lot of money.

Eventually I got tired of thinking, and I started to feel really hungry. "We have to stop and get something to eat," I said.

"Where?" She was looking blankly out a window.

"The nearest fast food place," I said.

She said, "You know that, by now, there's an A.P.B out for us and for this car."

"Wha——"

"An all points bulletin, Emilio. We're lucky it's nighttime. So if we have to stop and get something to eat, we'll have to park away from whatever place we find, and go in on foot."

"Okay," I said. I was thinking of the rental car, that, if the police were onto it, they'd be able to trace it to Sara from the documents she'd given to the car rental people.

"There's a Burger King over that hill," she said.

I pulled the Cobalt into the small parking lot and parked it in a dark corner, and we entered the little roadside franchise. I had a large double cheeseburger, a large fries, and a shake; she nibbled at some fries. She watched me eat. Any intimate feelings that had passed between us were long gone. Once more, she was serious as hell.

Back in the car, she drove and I fell asleep promptly. When I awoke, I was still groggy. A pinkish dawn was spreading over the desert. The California morning sun came up clear and hot. In the cloudless sky, the base of the distant mountains shimmered in the haze, their serrated peaks still stark and lonely against the morning sky.

Had I been paying attention I would have noticed the desert greasewood had given way to mesquite and bunch grass in that desolate terrain. The next road sign said that L.A. was still sixty miles away. It had been cold the night before, but the sun was promising a hot day. It was high in the sky when Sara pulled into a breakfast place. "I'm going to get a coffee and a muffin or something," she said. "Want anything?"

"Just a large coffee." She pecked me on the forehead as if I was her child and glided off.

I smiled and drifted back to sleep. It seemed like only a few minutes had passed, but when I opened my eyes again the sun was higher and the dashboard clock told me that she had been gone almost an hour. I settled back to wait, but thought better of it and twisted around to look at the back seat.

All of Sara's bags were missing.

I reached in to my backpack. *My God,* I realized. *She stole my money!* I sprinted into the restaurant to check for her. She was nowhere to be seen. I looked around and discovered a Greyhound station nearby and dashed back to the car, but I found a cop walking around it, weapon out, radio locked between the crock of the neck and his ruddy cheek.

I swore and slowed down. He had not seen me. I told myself that if he looked around and saw me—that if he thought I was suspicious looking, he'd order me to freeze, and I would surely be screwed because of the gun I had in my pocket. *Then what would Sara do?* I thought. *Reach for your gun, man!* A panicked voice in my head screamed, *Reach for your gun! It might come down to it being either you or him!* "No!" I hissed to myself. This couldn't be *happening*! I glanced around casually, not to arouse suspicion, and saw a van. I slipped behind it and began to head off towards the Greyhound station.

I was feeling crushed inside, my joy about helping my mother earlier than expected dashed. The only money I had on me was the two thousand dollars in my pocket.

I thought of Sara, suddenly glad that she had skipped out on me. If I hadn't suspected it, I would not have been looking for her in the restaurant and might still have been in the Cobalt waiting on her. That cop would have found me in it. Small mercies!

Then came squad car sirens and the squeal of brakes and the chatter of police radios. The cop who'd found the Cobalt had called in for backup. Soon they'd be swarming the area. I had to act nonchalant. *Think like a cop, Emilio!* I told myself. *What would you think?* I thought that the cash store robbers would try to make their escape on the bus and realized that continuing to head towards the Greyhound bus station was a bad idea. I turned my steps away from the bus station and went into the restaurant instead.

I bought a coffee and an egg-and-cheese on a bagel, and waited. Soon enough I saw a squad car rush by towards the bus station. I was going to sip that coffee until things got very quiet.

About an hour later, I tossed my gun into the garbage can outside the restaurant and entered the station, terrified that a cop would find me. I knew the weapon would tie me to Sara's crimes and Dustin. I bought a ticket for L.A., got comfortable in the bus seat, and began munching on the Doritos and sipping coffee I had bought for the trip, everything tasteless in my mouth.

CHAPTER **13**

I FELT BETTER AFTER I wired my father fifteen hundred dollars from a Western Union office at the bus terminal in Los Angeles. It wasn't enough, but it would buy my mother some time.

I found a pay phone and called him to let him know the money was on its way. He was excited, and though I thought he would ask where I'd gotten it, he didn't, just thanked me and said he would have the coyote meet in a few days at the Los Angeles Union terminal. He told me to call the next day for an exact date and time.

I found the number for the rectory Pedro and I had worked at in Phoenix, called, and spoke with Father Georgio. "Is he there right now?" I asked. Pedro was not, but the priest said he expected to see him in about an hour. I said I would wire him a hundred and fifty dollars for Pedro to buy a bus ticket to L.A., that his being in L.A. was important, that he needed to board a bus that day.

The priest thanked me for caring and said he'd make sure that Pedro got the money.

I was left with a little under three hundred bucks and only the clothes on my back.  Compared with what I had when I left Phoenix, though, I was somewhat grateful.  I knew I'd be able to buy a new backpack, two pairs of jeans, and a couple of T- shirts.  I was going to survive.  I found an inconspicuous little store and bought all of it.

So all I had to do until I met the coyote was kill time.

I found one of the parks in central L.A., a shady spot with lots of imported desert palms.  There were only a few people around, and I wanted mostly to rest, so I took a nap on a bench; I awoke and went hunting for lunch.  To stretch my money as far as I could, I found a McDonald's and ordered two cheeseburgers and a small soda from the dollar menu.  The hot meal tasted good—and gave me a chance to reflect.

I started to daydream about meeting the coyote.  I didn't know if he would put me on an eastbound bus the same week or what, but as the time passed I'd been getting less and less interested in going to New Jersey for a year of manual labor.  I wasn't lazy—it just seemed too long.  I wanted to get help to my mother as soon as I could.  Maybe a year would be too late.

I considered what Sara and I had done together.  Technically, we hadn't robbed the check-cashing place.  That money had fallen into our hands, literally.  I thought about the security cameras: We were probably on the tapes.  Would we come off as criminals or victims? We might not have been the actual thieves, but we *had* left with money that wasn't ours. But Sara'd shot a *cop*, and I'd been with her. I'm sure that would land me in jail. Who would believe my story?

The money I'd sent home would last a while, but when I calculated how long it would take to earn enough to pay off the coyote and buy the medicine, things began to look glum. If I could find Sara and get my forty-five thousand back, I could go straight home without working for months. The money belonged to me—I'd risked getting shot, forget thrown in jail. I was probably a wanted felon and had no idea if I'd even been identified. And there was the chance that, if Sara got caught, she'd turn me in.

It would be better to get the money and go home.

But how would I find her? I figured she was going along with the Sarin attack. If she tried to stiff them, a beautiful woman like her would have a tough time hiding. . .*though she could be with them right now,* I realized. I knew she had a fiendish demon boiling in her. *She shot a cop, man! How could I not have seen this coming?*

With night approaching, I called Father Georgio. He said Pedro would be at the bus terminal at seven the next morning. All I had to do was wait some more. I left the park and went for a walk down the city streets, looking for a church, a homeless shelter, an abandoned building, anywhere I could sleep and be reasonably safe. After three hours, I gave up and returned to the park.

When I got there, I spotted a large group congregated on the grass, holding candles and chanting something. I was curious, so I paused in the back next to a young white woman. She was wearing a black dress and a gray headband, and she had a sad look in her eyes. "Here, move in," she said. I did, and someone handed me a candle. I stood there swaying side to side, humming what I thought the words were. The service lasted for about a half hour before the woman turned to me and said, "Were you friends with Richard?"

"I-I'd just gotten to know him," I said.

She shook her head. "What a way to die. . . ."

"True," I muttered. "What a way to go."

"That a huge container at the port should crush anyone is just too much!" She said it with so much hurt, it brought on goose bumps.

"I'm so sorry," I said.

"Yeah, well, Richard loved this park. He's going to be missed."

The crowd began to move in an orderly fashion. I stayed in line and was led to a table of cookies and coffee. I had never met the dead man and had no business at his memorial service, but I stuffed my pockets with whatever cookies I could and grabbed a cup of coffee.

I hung out with them until around midnight, when a guy with a blue Ford F-250 pick-up pulled up on the grass. I helped him load the table, coffee pot, and bags of garbage. He was an older man, and I sensed that he was deeply heartbroken. When we were done, he nodded to me and said, "Thanks for the help."

I nodded back. "Anytime."

"You're new around here," he said.

"Uh, yeah."

"You live in the area?"

"I'm. . .kind of in transition right now."

"Where are you sleeping tonight, my friend?" he asked.

I blinked. I guess he read my mind, and laughed. "I've got a garage converted into living space with a stocked refrigerator and a bunk. There's even a computer if you like games." He winked. "You know."

I grinned.

"You're welcome to rest your backpack down a while, you know, spend the night," he said.

"Thank you."

We were the last to leave the park. The memorial service got me thinking about Arturo, Pedro's father, this Richard, and how tragically their lives had been cut short. More and more, I no longer wanted to go to New Jersey. I wasn't up to the trip; it no longer made sense.

I settled into the garage. His refrigerator was indeed stocked with lots to eat and drink, even cans of beer and a lot of Hungry Man dinners. He even had a microwave. I enjoyed myself. But before long I was thinking of Sara again and of what we had gone through. And of Julio and the Sarin gas plot.

There was a computer on a little desk in a corner, and I thought, Maybe I should do some research on this Sarin gas thing.

I learned, among other things, that Sarin gas has many names. It's called O-isoproply. Also methylphosphonofluro-idate, GB and others. It's a nerve gas and is colorless and odorless and kills upon contact. It can be moved in any air flow system, a ventilation duct, an air conditioning duct, almost any conveyance that moves air. It can be detected but usually not before it's too late. The victim suffers shortness of breath, nausea, and other symptoms leading to death.

I felt sick when I logged off.

I went to bed in the furnished garage of a stranger, a white man who seemed easygoing and kind, and thought of the red-bearded man who had shot Arturo, a white man, too. I shook my head as sleep came. You never know, I thought. Then I though of Sara and at some point she became Momma, and I fell off to sleep.

The next morning my benefactor came by the garage, and I thanked him for his hospitality. "I guess you're ready to hit the road."

"Yes," I said.

"Where are you from—*De donde esta usted?*"

I told him, and my name, and that a friend and I were looking for work. I had a little over a hundred dollars left and needed to make some money.

"Where's your friend?" he said.

"He's coming up from Phoenix. I'm going to meet him.

"I'm all for you Illegal guys."

Was I that obvious?

"I have work for you and your friend. I'm a contractor. I was going to leave here in a few minutes and go to the square to find four guys to do some roadwork. If you say you have a friend, then I'll just need two more guys, huh?"

"Cool. He has a broken hand, but he's no slouch," I said.

"It's okay. Tell you what, I'll give you a lift to pick up your friend, and then we'll try to find a couple more guys at the square—how does that sound?"

"Sounds good."

He stuck out his hand. "Call me, Greg," he said, "and tell you what. . .you and your friend can stay in the garage a while." He shrugged and added, "By the way, if you need to wash up, there's a shower unit through there, okay?"

"I can do that."

"Okay," Greg said. "I'll pick you up in twenty minutes."

I couldn't believe my luck.

We met Pedro at the bus terminal that bright, sunny morning. He got off the bus wearing blue jeans and a blue-and- white horizontally striped shirt, and he smiled when he saw me. "*Hola, mi amigo*," he said.

I threw my arm around him. "How you been?"

"Good, man, you know. Thanks for the ticket."

"It wasn't a big deal."

He was smiling again when he said, "*Gracias*."

I introduced him to Greg, and we drove off.

I had sent for Pedro because I didn't want him living on the streets. There I was, a wanted person, taking on the role of foster parent. Who the hell had I become?

Greg pulled up to a corner where about nine or ten young men had gathered. He rolled down his window. "I need two guys," he called out, and pointed down the boulevard. "We're fixing the sidewalk seven blocks from here. Sixty dollars each."

They all converged on the pick-up truck. Greg looked them over and pointed to two guys. They piled into the back of the truck. I saw a lot of dark eyes glaring at us as we pulled away.

He drove down La Cienega to where other men were waiting with hard hats, jackhammers, sledgehammers, and picks. The job was in front of a shoe store with a sign that read *Nine West*. We got out of the truck, and Greg handed Pedro and me a vest, a yellow construction helmet, and a flag. The other men had the same equipment, but with a sledgehammer.

Greg told me to stand on the corner and stop cars that were making a right turn on red so that people would be safe in the coned area set up for pedestrians while the sidewalk was being removed. It was simple. I had to watch the light and hold up cars that were trying to make a right at the red light. Pedro had his own station.

**B**y mid-morning, I was getting into it when I spotted a pair of familiar legs crossing the intersection. They were gorgeous, skirt up to the thighs.

She spotted me just as I saw her, and rushed back to her car down the street on a one-way block. She had to pass me, but I was frozen in place—luckily, Sara didn't take my toes off or run me over when she bolted out of there. And then she was gone. It'd happened so quickly, I didn't notice if she'd jumped the light.

But I *was* going to find her. And I *did* remember the car—a blue Ford Victoria with Nevada plates. A rental, maybe, since they often had out-of-state license plates on them. The Arizona one had

Nevada plates. *There must be a way to track that down,* I thought. But would she leave town by the time I did?

That night Pedro and I slept in the garage. The next day, I told Greg that I had something very special to do. I told Pedro the same. "I'll be back here later, *hombre. No te preoccupas.*"

I hit the street thinking about her. She would naturally need wheels. L.A. is a spread-out place, and it's hard to get around without them. I had a hunch that took me back to the bus station where I came in. She's come through here, too. It had an Enterprise-Rent-a-Car booth. I got the attention of the young woman manning it in a company uniform with a bright yellow scarf and a bright smile. I put a worried look on my face and said, "My girlfriend just called me. Her rental broke down at her apartment."

The girl said, "Oh, dear, I hate when that happens. What's your girlfriend's name?"

I said, "Sara." I hesitated and looked at her, hoping my eyes were pleading. A bit sheepishly, I said, "We, uh, just met, you know? To be honest, I haven't gotten around to her last name yet, but she's driving a blue Ford Crown Victoria. I don't want to call her and ask her last name."

The girl, a modern young lady I was sure, saw my dilemma. She hesitated, studied me, and probably decided I looked innocent enough. She punched some keys on the computer and said, "Driving a blue Ford Crown Victoria, we have a Sara Buchanan at the La Caya Apartments on La Brea."

"Yes. That's her. Do you have the apartment number correct?"

She said, "Apartment 23?"

"Yes, that's right.  How soon can she expect the tow truck?"

The girl punched some more keys and with a frown said, "I'm afraid it'll take at least two hours."

I said, "Fine.  And thanks very much."  She just smiled at me.

CHAPTER **14**

**L**A BREA IS A main drag and had public transportation. It took over an hour to get there, but I hoped I had at least another hour before the tow truck came. She knew I was looking for her, and if she was home, she wasn't about to open the door for me.

Sure enough, there was the Crown Victoria parked in the parking lot opposite Apartment 23. I was feeling like Sherlock Holmes, much pleased with myself.

I had a coffee at the convenience store across the street and watched the door. How could I get her out, or get me in? My mind was blank. All I could do was continue to watch her door.

I was startled when she came out a few minutes later. I wasn't ready for her. I knew I needed to get across the busy street and reach her before she locked herself into the car. The traffic slowed me down, and by the time I got across the street, she was wheeling out of the parking lot. Worse still, she had spotted me. I made a futile ten-yard chase, but soon I was left in her exhaust fumes. Panting, I went back to the convenience store. I hadn't noticed if she had her purse or any bags. If not, she'd have to come back for them, but that would mean me staking out the apartment 24/7, and that wasn't possible. I had blown it.

Back to the drawing board: All I had managed to accomplish was to flush her out and drive her deeper underground, where the chances of finding her would be even harder. With Dustin out of the picture, her only reason for being in L.A. would be to help Julio release the gas in the subway vents. If she didn't, he would kill her.

I got back to the garage later that evening. Pedro had a pocketful of candy to share with me. He even wanted to share what he'd been paid. I was more than touched.

It was starting to look, I thought as I sank onto the mattress, that there was no way I would get to Sara. There was a slim possibility that she would have to return the car at the bus station, and I could get to her there. But she was too clever for that. She'd park it out in the street and let them pick it up before she risked coming back anywhere I might be waiting.

Waiting was no answer anyway. I could no more afford to watch the bus station 24/7 as I could her apartment. Someone was bound to report anybody who looked like me hanging around with no ID.

On the one hand, how do I hook up with her so I could get some money? On the other, she was getting involved with killing thousands of people. I had this knowledge and had to act on it. It was a moral thing. I believed in God: I couldn't stand by and let thousands of His people be murdered. Yet to save myself, I had to. And by saving myself, I was saving Momma. With me in jail, she had no chance.

And then—and then!—I was falling for her and in some odd, stupid way hoped we could work something out and be together. Like the needy love-struck fool I was, during our lovemaking I thought she had felt something for me. I certainly had for her. But then I'm Latino, and, as any gringo will tell you, a sucker for love. These cold *Norte Americanos* were more oriented to money and the things it could buy.

I had always known that I had another alternative: Tell the cops about Sara, Julio, and their plan. But I couldn't walk into a police station. I'd been with her when she shot the cop, and I was an illegal. Who in the world would listen to me? How could I convince them? I could make an anonymous call, but there were probably so many of them that the chances of saving a single life were slim.

The next day I found myself in front of a computer screen at the Los Angeles Public library. I wanted to find out if the cop in Vegas had died. That was important. I looked for the newspaper for the day after the hold-up and learned that he had lived. He would recover. Surprisingly, both of Julio's henchmen were in stable condition. And in a lot of trouble.

I also needed to know more about Sara. I assumed that Buchanan really was her last name, since she'd rented the car and needed ID. She had told me that she grew up in a little town named

Hyder, in Yuma County, Arizona.

I looked up the town newspaper and went back to the year I believed she was born. I figured I could be off by as much as three years either way, so I had to cover six.

I was still working away in late afternoon when I came across a Sara Ralston, a member of the cheerleading squad of the local football team. In uniform, her legs were just as unforgettable. The picture was grainy and ten years old, but I believed it was her. She was easy to spot in the small high school graduating class.

Another article gave an account of her parents' death in a terrible car accident on a rain-swept Arizona highway when she was about fifteen. She, and her kid sister Katherine, had gone to live with their uncle, Joe Ralston. I went to the appropriate high school graduation date for Katherine Ralston and found her, too—as beautiful as her sister, with deep dimples in her cheeks. She was going to Arizona State University in Phoenix. I wondered how Sara, who certainly looked like a nice Arizona farm girl, had gotten mixed up with the likes of Dustin and agreed to build canisters of Sarin gas.

Though this wasn't much information, it humanized her a little, though she *had* told me, "In this life, you have to do what's best for yourself." It's a philosophy which implies "and to hell what happens to other people."

I checked the Phoenix papers to dig up more about Dustin. That didn't take long—I'd found the same stories in Las Vegas. There was one more detail: *Man Who Accidentally Shot Himself in Leg Is Doing Well*. Evidently old Dustin had pulled through. There was no mention of how well he was doing. I wondered if Sara had discovered this and could even now be heading for Arizona to stop him from helping Julio. Who knew?

I was back to my original problem: how to find her.

I thought about laying my hands on a "slim Jim," that thing thieves use to get into cars, maybe finding her car back at the motel and getting in the back seat. But it would be in broad daylight on a busy thoroughfare. Even if I managed to get in, she'd have her guard up and probably shoot me if she found me. No—I needed some way to get face to face with her without giving her the upper hand.

I left the library and began walking back to Greg's garage. On the way I disproved any notion that I thought best while walking. Nothing came to me. If I didn't find her in L.A., I would have no way to find her.

CHAPTER **15**

**T**HEN IT HIT ME.

At a drab bodega trying to look colorful, I got a few dollars' worth of quarters, found a phone, and got the number for Arizona State University in Phoenix. Kathy was the family obligation Sara had been talking about that night we drove in from Vegas.

I called the dormitory and asked for Kathy Ralston. Her roommate said she wasn't in, but that she'd be back in a half-hour. I reached her on the next call. "Yo, listen, babe," I said, "it's important to you and your sis."

"Who is this?" she asked. "I—"

"*I* do the talking, bitch. You call her right now and tell her to meet Dustin at the McDonald's at La Cienega and West 18th at six tonight. Tell her ol' Dustin's feeling *much* better now— and if she's thinking of not coming, tell her my boy Thomas is right down the street from your dormitory. He'll be visiting you. Ol' Thomas is good with a blade, very good, and he likes college girls, even more than me. You tell her that she better be there. And tell her that if I don't call Thomas back, he's ready to use that blade of his on you. He's already seen you. Pretty little thing, blonde braids. Dimples. You tell Sara that. No tricks, or Thomas'll be just dying to meet you."

Before she could protest, I hung up. Something told me Sara would have kept ol' Dustin from her sister.

I waited for her a few blocks away from the McDonald's. It was the longest three hours of my life. I made sure that I was about five minutes late. I wanted her to get anxious about her sister's fate.

When I showed up, she was looking nervous, but still as beautiful as ever in a pair of fitted slacks and a yellow T- shirt that hid none of her curves. When she spotted me, she looked like she was going to bolt. I stopped her, blocked her way. "I'm working with Dustin. Yeah, I called him. Had a nice chat. Looks like we have both concluded you're one lying, cheating bitch. . . . Don't be foolish. Your sister is still under the knife."

She looked at me incredulously. "You? You sissy. You?"

I smiled my most evil smile. She leaned back; but after a few moments' thought, she just didn't buy it. She tried to sneer, but it didn't quite work. "You? Working with Dustin? Who are you kidding?"

"You going to take that chance? Still think I'm dumb? I found Kathy, didn't I? I hooked up with Dustin, didn't I? I know if there's one thing you love in this world, it's your little sister. Why, you've taken care of her since she was a kid."

She looked at me more incredulously but said nothing.

I said, "Dustin is a psycho, and he'd kill people like I blow my nose. You want to take that chance with the girl?"

". . .What do you want?" she asked in a low snarl.

"My forty-five thousand."

"You don't want it *all*?" She seemed genuinely surprised.

My contempt at that moment was so fierce I could have strangled her. "No," I said icily, slow and even, trying to control myself. "I know it's hard for your greedy brain to wrap around, but not everybody's like you."

She nodded and said, "Okay. I'll do what you want."

"Like I believe you. Just like that. There are a couple more conditions. You and I are going to be real tight until I get the money. Also, if I find out that you went ahead with the attack, I'm going to the cops. I'm going to identify you. Buchanan isn't your name, Ralston is. So the cops will know all about you and your sister. It won't take them too long to find you, unless you spend some money on plastic surgery. You won't be too hard to find."

Her jaw dropped. "You. . .you—"

"What? Bastard? You think I'm a bastard? You pick me up, get me involved, I share the dangers with you, you even make love with me. And then you dump me, steal my money, and *you* call *me* a bastard? I don't think so, babe."

She bristled but said nothing.

"Now, where's the money, and when do I get it?"

She remained silent for a few moments. "You don't think I carry it *around* with me, do you? It's stashed, and there's no way to get it until tomorrow."

"Oh, sure. You're using a bank." I gritted my teeth. "If you don't tell me where the money is, I can probably get enough off your dead body to take care of me. Then I'll be happy to tell Dustin where your sister is."

I could almost see the wheels of her mind working. I was just getting warmed up. All the days and nights of frustration thinking about her had my juices flowing. "Let me see," I went on. "I've seen my share of American movies. Isn't this where you tell me how we can screw Dustin and go away together with all the money, yours and his and mine?"

She frowned, almost looked sad, but I was in no mood for soft looks and real emotion. She practically spat, "You don't know any-thing about *me*, my *life*, what I've *been* through."

"No, I don't, and I don't give a shit either. Where's the money?"

She reached for her purse, and I grabbed her arm. She said, "I'm just getting the bank receipt to show you." She retrieved a safety-deposit document from an L.A. branch of Chase Bank.

"So? What does this prove, that you have a vault? You could have anything in it."

"Believe what you want."

I said, " I believe I'll tell Dustin to go ahead and have fun with little Kathy."

Her head snapped up at that. "*Why?* I'm telling you the *truth*. You'll find out soon enough, tomorrow morning."

I sucked on a tooth. ". . .Why would you use a bank?"

"Because the cops might be looking for me. My alias isn't that solid. Just a simple ID. They may be able to find out who I am on their own. I. . .I do have a record."

I considered that. Nothing she'd said *didn't* make sense.

She was still talking. "I didn't want to leave it in the motel. Lots of keys get passed around. Somebody could steal it. I figured a bank is safer."

"Well, you're right, I guess. I'll find out in the morning. So," I said, "it looks like it's just you and me. Just like old times."

She said, "Okay, let's go. I've got a motel room nearby."

I grabbed her purse and fished around until I found her pretty little .32, which I slipped into my pocket. I found about two thousand bucks, too, which I grabbed as well. "Down payment," I said.

"Yeah, right."

"Just like a thief," I fired back, sarcasm dripping off the words. "Because you are, you think everybody is.. . . Lead the way, babe."

Her car was nearby, and she drove to a motel. I had her use the key while I stood off to the side and out of the line of fire if somebody was waiting inside."

"Boy," she said, "you've become real cautious since the last time I saw you."

"I've been screwed over a lot since then, and I've learned my lesson. Especially with you."

Once we were in the room, I checked the bathroom and the closet as well as under the bed. "Seems silly, doesn't it? But I wouldn't put anything past you."

I pulled the belt off her robe and the ties off the rear window curtain. "What are you going to do with those?" she asked, looking worried.

"I'm not going to stay up all night watching you," I said, and motioned her to the bed. Reluctantly, she lay down, and I tied her hands to the bed posts. I also found some pills in a bottle in her carryall. "What are these?" I asked.

"Sleeping pills."

"Oh, yeah," I said, shaking out a couple. "You might need them. Help you sleep."

"And if I don't take them?"

"Then I gag you too, and tie your legs as well."

Looking resigned, she stuck out her tongue and I fed them to her. I lay back and watched TV. She fell asleep first.

She was doing what I said, but, I figured, one wrong word and I could blow the whole plan.

In the morning I went out for a couple of breakfast sandwiches and coffee. When I came back, she was awake. I untied her and laid her coffee and sandwich on the night table. She rubbed her wrists and looked at me. It wasn't a glower, nor did she frown. Her look was soft, but I didn't trust her, though I wanted to deep down. I had already made that mistake.

CHAPTER **16**

**S**HE HEADED FOR THE bathroom. I said, "Wait a minute." I went in, and checked. There was a window. "Leave the door open."

She gave me an insulted look, but went in and showered. I lay on the bed, watching her. She came out naked with a towel turbaned on her head. She padded around the room as if she were alone. I hated the stirring in my loins but told myself it was libido, nothing more.

Before we left for the bank she said, "Can I call Kathy and tell her everything is cool? She must be worried sick."

"Does she know where you are?"

"No," she said. I would have to be more careful: If the girl knew, she could bring the cops down on me, though Sara was in deeper than me.

I told her to call. She sat at the edge of the bed and crossed her legs, still naked. ". . .Hi, babe. It's me. Look, I know you're worried, but don't. Everything's cool." She paused. "Don't cry, Kathy. I *said* everything's going to be okay. Have I ever lied to you? . . . Yes, it's going to be all right. We'll get the restaurant, and we'll be together. Like I promised. So chill out and wait to hear from me. It won't be long."

By the time she got dressed, it was nine o'clock. We set out for the bank. When we got there, I yanked at the door handle, but it was locked. A sign on the door read *Closed for the Holiday*.

"Holiday?" I said.

She sighed. "It's Thanksgiving Day."

I glanced at her. "When were you going to tell me?"

With a saucy look on her face that she seemed to enjoy, she said, "I forgot."

"Looks like we're going to be able to extend our honeymoon a bit longer."

I had her drive to Greg's garage, where Pedro was staying. We parked and honked the horn. It didn't take long before he came strolling out. He spotted me.

I said, "Get in the back seat."

He did. "Hi, Miss Sara," he said.

She smiled. "Hi, baby."

I turned around and handed him a thousand dollars in cash. "I probably won't see you after today, so I want to give you this and say *adios, amigo*. I'm sorry I brought you here only to leave you, but it's important."

He looked at the money and back at me, obviously stunned,

and murmured, "*Gracias, mi amigo.  Gracias.*  I hope things work out for you."  He kept shooting glances at her, confused, I guess, to see me with her and the money.  "How did—"

"*Adios, amigo.*"

"*Si, si.  Y tu tambien, amigo.*  You, too.  *Vaya con dios.*"  We shook hands, and he was gone, still gazing at the money in his hand.

We returned to the motel, grabbed our bags, and checked out. I wasn't leaving anything to chance—I didn't know if she'd already told her sister where we were staying.  We checked into another motel and settled down to wait out the day, she on one bed, I on the other.  We managed to say nothing all day long.  I had Italian food sent in for dinner so that we didn't have to leave.  Out in public, I was always worried.  I had her .32 in my pocket, and I stayed behind her, constantly worried that she'd realize I could never shoot her if she ran or called for help.

It seemed like the next day would never come, but it did.  We got the money.  I waited in the lobby while the clerk escorted Sara downstairs to the vault.  She could still rat me out.  I was worried. When she came back she said, "I want to get a cashier's check and send it to my sister."  I had no objections—in fact, I did the same, sent $9,800.00 home in an envelope and stamp the bank provided. We returned to the motel, checked out, and loaded our bags into the car.

I put her behind the wheel and said, "Drive."

"Where to?"

"Take the Interstate east.  We're going to Tucson."

"Why?"

"Just *drive*," I said.  On the way out of town we picked up breakfast sandwiches and coffee, and ate as we drove, that morning routine becoming familiar, and there's something to be said for familiar things.

Before we reached the Arizona border Sara said, "If you're taking me out of the Sarin thing, I don't know if you know it, but all you're going to do is get me killed."

I said, "Why? You're that committed? They can't do it without you?"

"No to both questions.  But they're planning it around some significant date in the life of Emiliano Zapata.  If that date passes, they lose some of the publicity impact."

"You tell me why he won't just snuff you in the end. You shot his boy."

"You don't *get* it, Emilio.  Everything stays cool if I hold up my end of the deal.  I have a meeting with him in two days."  She paused, her lips pressed together, before she added flatly, "You do realize you're going to get me killed, yes?"

I didn't say anything.  I thought about it.  I thought of nothing else.  She could be lying; it was a way of life with her.

Couldn't they find somebody else to distribute it in the ventilation system?  And how does whoever puts the canister in place escape in time?

That night, we checked into a motel outside Tucson and ate in the dining room. As we lay on separate beds, doing our usual motel room routine of watching TV, she said, "So you've found yourself a little brother."

"Pedro?"

"Yeah.  Someone you feel you needed to help along."

"He helped me, and I like to think I'm a grateful person."

"So maybe you'll walk a mile in my shoes before you decide to be so judgmental with me."

In the morning, as she was buckling her seatbelt, I said, "We're taking Interstate 131 South."

She turned to me. "South? There's nothing south but Mexico."

"South," I said.

"So that's what it is! You're going home, and you need me to drive."

I said nothing.

She said, "You should get yourself a phony ID. You walked in. You're going to go through a border checkpoint now.  You need *something*."

She was right.  She saved me the embarrassment of asking her what I should do by driving to the seediest part of downtown.  I didn't stop to wonder how she knew where it was.

We went into a bar and sat down for a drink.  After checking out everybody there, she motioned to the big, burly bartender.  He came over. "You know anybody who can help him out?" she asked, motioning to me. "We want to head south."

The bartender said, "I *might* know somebody."

She slid a fifty across the bar.  He covered it with his palm and started wiping the bar with a grungy-looking towel.  "Guy comes in about noon every day. Tall, stringbean.  Usually wears jeans, a straw Stetson, and a black string tie."

It was eleven-thirty, so we had a couple more beers and listened to the Country Western music. When the guy came in, the bartender motioned toward him.

An hour later we had a picture ID driver's license for me as well as a birth certificate that said I'd been born in Union City, New Jersey.

By mid-afternoon we had crossed the border into Mexico.

C H A P T E R **17**

**B**EFORE LEAVING TUCSON, I had bought a state-of-the-art laptop, prompting Sara to joke, "You going to watch porno on the boring trip?"

I'd said nothing. So far it had been her who warned me of the problems of crossing the border without an ID. Frankly, I'd had no plan whatsoever for how to do that. I *had* realized that things would go smoother with her driving—her ID would stand up better than my phony one. Lots of illegals had those, and if an official really wanted to check, mine wouldn't bear much scrutiny.

The land we passed through was pretty arid, like the deserts of the American Southwest. I knew that, later on, we would reach the valleys of the Sierra Madre on our way to Mexico City. I figured that it would take two or three days to reach El Salvador. Once there, I was prepared to let her go.

Before we reached Nogales, she again began talking about her problem. "I wasn't just yanking your chain back there about Julio killing me. These are ruthless people."

I rolled my eyes. "What good would that do them?"

"You don't get it, do you? He'd kill me just to send out a warning that you don't screw with him. He's going to gas a *whole subway system*. And all he hopes to get out of that is some *publicity*."

I glanced at her. She did have a more practical criminal mind than I, but then she was a pro. I said, "You should have thought about that before you signed up for the job."

"Righteous sonofabitch, aren't you? Like you haven't already taken stolen money. Like you aren't ready to kill for your family back home!"

"So? What's your point? That I'm a hypocrite?"

"You said it. Not me."

*Now who was being self-righteous?* I snapped, "I would *never* go out and kill innocent people to get money! All I've done is take money from a *store*, money that's probably insured anyway. . . . And by the way," I added, "that cop that you shot in Vegas didn't die. You just saved yourself a life sentence, or worse, if you get caught."

"I know. Didn't you think I checked? . . ." She glanced at me out of the corner of her eye. "Surprised?"

I didn't answer, afraid that I might again fall under her spell and do even more stupid things. "And Julio's henchmen are alive and well," I said.

Around dusk we pulled into Nogales. I wanted the anonymity of a motel but needed the Internet connection of a larger place, so we found a nice hotel downtown.

I hooked up and found some information on Emiliano Zapata, the Mexican revolutionary the current movement glorified. There were two significant anniversary dates in his story-one when, along with Pancho Villa, he marched into Mexico City at the head of an army and took a seat behind the president's desk in the palace, the other when he declared a peasant revolution to overthrow the corrupt government and restore land reforms. Both dates were only a week or so away.

Sara sat on the bed, disinterested in my research. I turned to her. "You have no idea when this is going to happen?"

"No."

"So why were you and your people all heading for L.A. at the same time?"

She said nothing.

I sat staring at the blank screen, wondering what to do next. She walked up and stood behind me. I had been cautious with her. I had the gun, and I didn't dare let her get behind me and hit me over the head with something. But I was tired and had let my guard down. She stood there, clicked on the screen, and read the info.

"It's next week," I said, "isn't it?"

Her voice was flat. "If they get somebody else to do what Dustin or I was going to."

I looked up the L.A. FBI office and composed an email to the chief agent in charge. I gave him everything I had, sketchy as it was.

I didn't send it.  I planned to just before we left the hotel. . .or maybe, I thought, I'd be better if I waited until I was in El Salvador. If I did it now, they could track me down through the Mexican authorities before we got to El Salvador.  I deleted the message.

She was watching me like a hawk.

Rather than go out in public and give her a chance to slip away or get someone's attention, I ordered in again: I had to be prudent if I expected to make it home with all that money.

She asked, "I need a good shot of a decent bourbon.  Help me sleep.  How about it?"

I'd enjoyed one myself—but she was right.  I needed her to sleep. As it was, I was feeding her sleeping pills and tying her hands.

"Okay.  What do you want?"

"Have them send up a fifth of Chivas Regal, some ice, and some mix.

When the food and liquor arrived, I had no intention of having one.  But food went down better with a drink, so after she had three, I succumbed and had one.  It went a long way to easing the tensions.

Sitting on the bed, she was a little buzzy when she leaned forward, her hair falling over her eyes.  Her voice was a little slurred, too.  She looked at me through the tent of her brown hair, her eyes inquisitive.  "I suppose you think you're better than me."

"Why?" I asked.

"Because you gave that kid money, and you're only stealing to save your mother."

"I didn't say that.  I have my own reasons for what I do."

"You think I'm scum because I steal to better myself."

I took a sip of my drink. "I didn't say that."

"No. But you think it. . . . Why do you think I made it with you back in the States?"

It was my turn now to turn curious eyes on her. "I don't know. Suppose you tell me."

"Because I think I was falling for you. You didn't have to stick with me, but you did." I know she saw the skepticism in my eyes. "Tell me you didn't like me when we first met."

"I would never say that. Besides, what difference does that make, considering what you did?"

"And what *did* I do? You're a man. You don't have to face what I do."

"And what's that?"

"Men. Men grabbing after me all the time. Everyone's the same. When all I want to do is work, they give me a job so they can later get it on with me. Like that bastard Dustin. He raped me last year."

"Dustin is the kind of person you have chosen to associate with."

"What a holier-than-thou bunch of crap."

She took another drink and, without realizing it, I had another, too. She propped up some pillows against the headboard and sat up, stretching her beautiful legs in front of her, not bothering to pull down her bunched-up dress, now thigh high. She said, "I have to take care of my kid sister and get along in this world."

Not bothering to veil my sarcasm, I muttered, "And there are no jobs for Americans. It's much like it is in El Salvador—pick bananas or coffee in the fields for a few dollars a day. Oh, I see."

Her tone got whiney. "Hey, man, just because everything isn't as bad as it is in your country doesn't mean it's all *gravy* for us north of the border. I've been on my own for a lot of years now, and I'm determined to raise my kid sister so that she has a chance in life."

I sipped my drink and raised my glass to her. "I salute your noble intentions."

I think she thought I was completely genuine. I wasn't, but I did feel a bit different about her. She said, "Do you mean it?"

"Why not? Who am I to judge? As you pointed out, I'm just as much a criminal as you are now."

She put her glass down. "Baby," she cooed, "don't hate me. Make love to me like you did before. All sweet and tender. All soft and so tantalizing," she said, stretching her arms over her head. Her breasts rose with the gesture.

I got up and moved to the other bed, feeling righteous. And hollow. She looked irritated.

Just before dawn, I awoke from a fitful sleep. Sara was asleep, curled in the fetal position. She looked cold. I got an extra blanket out of the closet.

As I covered her, she stirred, murmuring, her eyes still closed. As I tucked in the blanket around her, her eyes opened sleepily to a squint and then wide and held mine. With my eyes deep in hers, she slipped out of her dress, got under the covers and held the blanket open, inviting me. I got out of my clothes and joined her, my lips hungrily seeking hers. She sighed softly. With lips parted, we explored each other's lips, wet tongues swimming back and forth, thrilling us. Finally we melted together, her body velvety soft, hair smelling of sunshine and shampoo.

After we had explored every detail, every hollow and plane of each other's faces, I lowered my head to her breasts. I kissed and sucked at the stiff nipples with a passion that left her huffing. She squirmed, eagerly urging me on. We made love until the sun brightened the windows. I finally fell asleep, my body behind her spooned to her soft curves.

It was awkward in the morning. At first I thought I had had a dream until I saw her face, sleepy and content. I still didn't trust her, although the previous night had gone a long way toward that. I suppose if getting away was her idea, she didn't act on it. She had access to the money, the car, all that she needed. But she was still here. And I was confused.

I don't think I acted differently toward her that morning, but by midday it seemed that the animosity between us had at least mellowed, and I was more confused than ever.

We ate our breakfast sandwiches with coffee in the car as she drove south. At the next rest stop I took over. I know for her, as well as me, the gesture evinced a small measure of renewed faith in her.

We were almost to Hermosillo when I told her that I needed a pit stop real bad. I spotted a bus station ahead. A bus pointing north was loading. As I got out, I snatched the keys out of the ignition. "Do you need a rest stop?"

"No. I'm good."

When I came back, she was gone, so I walked back. Maybe

she'd changed her mind about the rest stop. I waited for ten minutes outside the ladies room door until I began to get nervous. I asked a lady to see if my wife was in there. She came out a few minutes later and said, "Not unless your wife is elderly."

I dashed to the car. The parking lot was empty. The bus had left. With my heart in my mouth, I checked the back seat. Her money was gone. I checked my back pack. My money was there. I sat back and wondered if I shouldn't just drive on home myself. If I kept to the speed limit and drove carefully, I was only a day and a half or so away. Maybe, I told myself, it was meant that we split this way.

I thought about it some more before turning the car north. I would catch up with her in Nogales. It took less than an hour to spot the slow-moving bus. At the next rest stop, about fifteen minutes later, I asked the driver if I could come aboard. I had to give my wife a message. He agreed.

But she wasn't on the bus: I had been fooled yet again. She'd headed south, the very direction she had resisted going in with me. I turned the car around and headed for Mexico City. It was the only place that made sense.

I got there early the next morning, having pushed on through the night. I figured I must be getting close to the bus since I'd never stopped and the bus had to. It took a while to consider another possibility—that maybe she hadn't *caught* a bus.

I wasn't going to find her the way I found her in L.A., either. Mexico City was the largest city in the world. But the airport!—

she was going to get a flight home, or to San Francisco or who knows where. She probably already had. But I had to at least check.

I had a hard time negotiating the complicated traffic pattern at the airport. Eventually I found my way to International Departures. I parked the car, went in, and checked the monitors for northbound flights. The next AeroMexico flight to the States wasn't for four hours. Continental had one in three hours. American had one leaving in fifty-three minutes.

I found her at the customs counter, arguing with the agent about her ID. I stood aside. The agent was telling her in English that she didn't have the proper card, and that she would have to wait for the supervisor.

When she turned around, I was standing there. I said, "What a coincidence, running into you here." I put my hand in my pants pocket.

She glared at me. "Why should I go with you? I could start screaming, and you'd wind up in jail. And cut the shit with the hand in the pocket. You're not going to shoot me."

I said, "You're right. Why did you run? I kind of—"

"Oh, sure. Like I'm supposed to believe that, when we got to El Salvador, you wouldn't take my money, too."

"*That's* what you think?"

"Yeah. *That's* what I *think*. You've never seen that much money in your life."

"That's true."

"I just want *out*. I want to go *home*. And I didn't take your money. I could have, but I didn't."

"That's true, too." No small thing to her, considering what she's already done for that money and what her family obligations were. Every instinct in her would compel her to take the money again and run.

"Look," I said. "I'll tell you what. So that you don't have to be worried about me or anyone taking your money, why don't you wire it all home? Then you have no more problems."

She gazed at me, her eyes searching deep. ". . .Why did you follow me, if you aren't after my money?"

"I. . .well, I guess it's because I need you."

"To drive you home?"

"That, too."

She gazed at me some more. Then she said, "Let's go."

I said, "To the Bank of Mexico? There's an office here at the airport."

"No. To the car."

Mexico City has one of the highest populations on earth, and it was congested. It took a long time to get from the airport and onto the road that skirted the city, and again we headed south toward Santa Cruz. We were quiet. I was deep in thought. On a quiet stretch of road, I hung an abrupt U-turn and started north.

She looked at me intently, raised her sunglasses, and set them on her head. "What are you doing?"

"We've got to settle this Sarin thing. If you don't want to, you're free to go, but I have to go back. And when I get there, I'm bringing Pedro home with me."

After a few miles she said, "Are you doing this because you're a good person or for me?"

I finally said, "I don't really know. Maybe both. All I know is, I can't leave it up to chance whether thousands of people die, and I could have prevented it. Or—"

"Because they're going to get you for it. The only way out is to get them caught. That solves both problems. Mine and yours."

With a day and a half of travel ahead of us, I started her talking about herself by asking, "Did you really live on a ranch?"

"Yep. Everybody back home did some ranching. I did everything from rope calves to castrate bulls."

"After your parents died, you went to live with your uncle, right?"

"How did you know that?"

"Doesn't matter. How did you get along with your uncle?"

". . .Not very good. My dad wasn't real close to his brother, and when it turned out that he was our only living relative, he took me and my sister in unwillingly."

"So you moved in with your uncle?"

"Yeah. My sister was just a little kid, and she was lost without her parents, especially my mother. So I had to take her place. I did the best I could for Kathy, but she grew up insecure, scared, and dependent on me for, like, *everything*. Right now she's scared to death about what's going on with me. I promised her we'd go to San Francisco and open a restaurant. She could help me run it and go to school there. I think you can understand that, considering what you're doing for your mother."

"I do," I said.

"You don't seem to."

"Maybe my commitment isn't as strong as yours."

"Oh, I doubt that.  I think I'm just tougher than you."

I wanted to say, *If you consider ruthlessness being tough*, but I didn't. "In any case, since you have no interest in saving the good people of Los Angeles, you can still get Julio caught and off your trail."

"That's true—but I'd prefer he was out of the way permanently."

I said, "Well, I'm not going to murder anybody for you. That's for sure."

"I didn't ask you to."

We drove in silence all the way to the border, and when we found a motel in Tucson, we both went to bed and slept soundly.

In the morning, I reached my hand over to her side of the bed and felt only sleep warm sheets.  I jumped up and dashed to the bathroom. The door was closed.  Just then it opened, and Sara was standing there in her underwear, brushing her teeth.  She rinsed her mouth and offered me her lips. "Morning, babe."

I pecked back, feeling guilty. We got dressed, and after a quick motel dining room breakfast, headed west to L.A.

The royal palms of the oceanfront Pacific Palisades Hotel in Santa Monica were casting long shadows as we drove up the long driveway.  She said, "Ritzy."

I grinned. "What's the sense of having money if you can't spend it?"

Hand in hand, we skipped into the lobby almost like a pair of honeymooners. We took long showers, changed and went downstairs to a candlelight dinner, complete with a wonderful red wine that had a sweet aroma and bold taste.

She gazed at me over her wine glass, grinned, and said, "I bet you take all the girls to fancy places like this."

I returned the grin, feeling lighthearted for the first time in a long time. "You want to know a secret?"

Her eyes brightened eagerly. "Yeah?"

"I've never been in a place like this."

"In the States?"

"No, never. Anywhere."

She just stared while I searched for some understanding between us, something that maybe wasn't obvious but was there. I don't know if I found it. I did know that we had an absolutely total evening. It wasn't only the wine and the food and the ambiance, it was us. We seemed genuinely interested in us. I was a skeptic by nature—and with Sara, being skeptical was an imperative—but my current nature wanted to very much believe my instincts.

We made love most of the night until exhaustion took over. Morning would be soon enough to figure out the next step.

CHAPTER **18**

$\mathbf{T}$HE NEXT MORNING, THE sun was slanting in through the blinds, and the dust motes danced merrily as if to signal a good day. I opened the blinds to a sweeping vista. The Pacific Ocean, shimmering like a million diamonds, stretched away to the horizon. I eagerly awoke Sara. She whined a bit. "I want to sleep."

"Look at the beautiful day. Let's buy bathing suits and have breakfast by the pool. And then a dip in the ocean."

She turned to face me, her hair tousled. "What are you, the social director?" But she was grinning. She scissored her long legs out of the bed and padded to the bathroom. I was amazed at her genuine naturalness. Most women would have wrapped themselves in a sheet or something. She was as comfortable naked as she was dressed. I had never met a woman who so lacked inhibitions. It made me feel that way myself. And she had no pretensions, never pretended or tried to act like anybody but herself.

After a breakfast as elegant as it was delicious, we bought swimsuits at the hotel gift shop and went down to the beach. Hand in hand we headed for the surf. For the next hour and a half we frolicked like a couple of slick seals.

Later we sat by the pool enjoying the hotel's excellent service. We watched wealthy Americans do the same. Beautiful women in skimpy swimwear were everywhere. Some weren't with men their own age, but much older. I commented on it. Sara smiled and said, "Now you're beginning to see the American way."

I thought that was pretty cynical, but I wasn't feeling benevolent to America. Except for Pedro, who wasn't a gringo, the only Americans I had recently met, aside from Greg, had been murderous criminals. I didn't know where I fit Sara into that scheme; I didn't think it was true of *all* Americans.

The next afternoon, as we were sipping tall, cool drinks, she asked, "Have you forgotten why we came back?"

"No." I had instantly grown serious.

"Do you have anything in mind?"

"Not yet. I've put off thinking about it."

"Enjoying the good life?"

"Yes. It's as simple as that."

She said, "While I *have* been thinking about it, all I've come up with is the negative part."

I said, "Tell me."

She squirmed a bit on her lounge chair. She said, "The only

thing. . . . Excuse me if I think of myself first, but the only thing that's going to save me is if Julio gets caught. Don't forget, I blew them off for the second time—committed the ultimate betrayal."

"But they got the gas, and they paid for it. How is that a betrayal?"

"You *know* it wasn't the whole deal. The gas is pretty much useless to them unless they know how to release it into the subway vent system."

"They can't get someone else?"

"It may be too late. If they don't do it on Zapata's date, it's pretty much useless as a PR stunt. And one other thing: I'm the one who can tie him in with the purchase of the Sarin. Not to mention he could get the money back."

I thought about that. She was right. "But we have a general idea when they plan to strike—maybe we can tip off the FBI."

"We've been over that, babe," she said, her tone a bit dull, as if she were dealing with an unwilling child. And she was right. I just wanted the whole thing to go away, but I knew I couldn't live with the consequences.

I thought a while. "But if we give the FBI the date, can't they shut down the subway system?"

She smiled. "This is America, babe. Do you realize the economic chaos that would cause? Thousands of people not able to get to work. The bus system wouldn't be able to handle it. No. It would be a mess. Why, 9/11 shut this country down for months economically. If the government didn't bail out the airlines, they would have gone bankrupt being shut down for just a week."

"And," she added, "The FBI would never do anything without something more substantial than an anonymous phone call. They get hundreds—no, thousands—of them. They couldn't possibly shut down the country on the basis of any of them. And as you can see, most of those tips are phony, hoaxes from nuts. We're right back where we started."

I set my lips tight. "I didn't come back to fail. I can't sit by and watch such a catastrophe happen."

Oddly, her observations mirrored mine. "Funny you're so determined to save people who can't be much from your point of view."

"We're all God's children." I thought that was a bit melodramatic after I said it, yet it's exactly how I felt.

It wasn't until that night, over dinner, that she leaned forward confidentially and whispered, "The only way we're going to get what we both want is either get rid of Julio or steal the gas back."

I probably didn't realize how wide my eyes popped open. She looked at me and said, "Unless you have another or a better idea."

"Kill Julio?"

She grimaced. "It wouldn't be like killing Mother Teresa."

I let that sink in. It still didn't sit any better. "What about stealing the gas back? Is that possible?"

She shrugged. "We have three or four days to figure it out. The way I see it, if we find Julio, we find the gas."

I thought about that. As much as I was falling in love with her, I still didn't trust her. If the option was to kill a man who could ruin her life, I had a feeling that she wouldn't hesitate. This view of her didn't fit well with my new romantic image of her and us, but I knew I had to consider it. "You have any idea," I ventured, "how we can find Julio?"

She grinned. "None."

I dropped my head into my hands just as the waiter served the wine but immediately resumed my role of the attentive lover. When he left and we were sipping wine, she looked over the rim of her glass at me. There was a silly grin on her face.

I asked, "What?"

"You found me. And I would consider that pretty difficult. But you found a way. Let's put our minds to work here. There has to be a way to find him."

After a few more sips of the wine, my lips a little numb; I said, "You have no number for him, and you know none of his associates?"

She shook her head. "I did, but I tossed it in Mexico. Besides, calling him now would be suicide."

"You told me he's a dishonored member of the Frente Revolutionario, right?"

"Right."

"But he's *doing* this for the Frente."

"Right."

It made no sense. We knew we only had a few days before the disaster hit L.A., yet the allure of the beautiful hotel and endless blue ocean drew us. I wanted to forget about L.A. and Sarin gas and Julio and my mother, all of it, just wanted to swim in the ocean and feel the sun on my body. . .and to reach for the softness of this woman.

The next day, we were sitting on lounge chairs only a few feet from the surf, which roared ashore and curled in foaming white water almost to our toes. "Tide's coming in," she said aimlessly.

"The eternal."

"What?"

"The tide," I said. "It's eternal. Whether we're here or not, it'll keep coming in till the end of time. If there is an end to time."

She went quiet. "I never thought of that, but it's true. We come and go, and this right here at our feet will still be coming in when we're barely a memory."

I smiled. "We're getting so profound."

An attractive couple strolled by, feet in the surf in front of us. The girl, a sun-kissed California blonde, was wearing the latest bikini—a thong and a string. The guy was tanned and muscular. He had the six-pack that the Americans loved. He looked like an Olympic athlete. Sara commented, "She's going to need to keep up her Brazilian with a bikini that small."

I cocked my head. "Her Brazilian?"

Sara grinned. "Bikini line?"

I still didn't get it.

We were back pool-side having lunch when I stopped eating and gazed at her. "You said you'd agreed to meet Julio a few days ago, right?"

"Yes, why?"

"Where'd he want to meet you?"

"He said the Union Terminal."

"You have any idea why he picked it last week?"

She continued chewing on her shrimp cocktail. "No," she said. "Central location, I guess. Why?"

I didn't answer, my mind churning over. Eventually I said, "A guy like Julio doesn't maintain that build unless he's at the gym almost every day, right? Far as I know, men like that are in the habit of working out a lot. They can't let much time go by without it, they're so addicted to the rush."

"So?"

"Why not stake out a gym or two near Union Terminal?"

She thought about it. "I guess. But isn't that kind of a long shot?"

"What other shot do we have? We have the better part of this afternoon left. Let's see if we can find any gyms near the Union Terminal."

The shadows were growing long by the time we located one. I'd be the least recognizable to Julio, so I went in. When I came out, I said, "He's not there. But I think we should check out other gyms in the vicinity, and stake one out."

"Okay."

We had taken the precaution of bringing our stuff, as meager as it was, so we didn't have to go all the way back to Santa Monica. We found a reasonably clean motel close by and checked in.

I found a restaurant nearby, and we sat down to dinner. I asked, "Is Julio a man of means?"

"Does he have dough? I guess so. He came up with the money for the gas. But I don't really know. He doesn't look like a bum, if that's what you mean."

"In the morning, I want to keep an eye on a place I think he'd be most comfortable in. I'm sure there are at least a couple around. What do you think?"

She sipped her Tequila Sunrise. "You think like a damn cop."

In the morning we continued to sweep the terrain and found two gyms that looked alright. "This is a problem," I said. "We don't have much time, and if we watch the wrong gym, we're going to miss him."

She shook her head. "If *I* cover one, he's bound to make me."

I agreed. We went back to the motel disheartened.

At breakfast the next morning, I was about to say something when I put my coffee cup down and said, "Come on." She was surprised, but she followed me out to the car. We got in, and I drove to Greg's garage where Pedro was staying. I got out of the car and spotted him just as he was emerging from the garage. He looked stunned when he saw me. "*Mi amigo!*" he cried, throwing his arms around me.

He had a lot of questions, which I avoided as we walked back to the car. "Pedro, I need a favor from you."

He saw Sara. He said, "Ah, Miss Sara. You're back?"

I said, "Yes, but the favor—I need you to watch for a man at a gym across town."

"*Sí, sí. Como no?* For you, amigo, I do it."

I aimlessly re-introduced him to her. He was as enraptured as any fifteen-year-old boy could be.  But he said, "*Pero, hombre, I* introduced you to *her*."  He was right, but he still offered her his hand. "*Hola, senorita*."

She smiled.  "*Hola,* Pedro."

Before we got to the gym, I stopped at a clothing store and bought him a complete new wardrobe, from T-shirt to Addidas pants, Nikes and socks.  He needed to look like he was there to work out.  He was pleased with his new outfit.  We dropped him off; even with his new clothes, he couldn't hang out for long without them kicking him out, so I gave him two hundred bucks to sign up.  That way he could be working out, and hanging out, all day.  I handed it to him.  He asked, "It will cost so much?"

"Keep the rest for yourself."  Sara was able to describe Julio better than I; he had a few distinguishing marks—a scar under his left eye he'd gotten in his wars with the Frente against the government, and tattoos on one arm.

We drove over to the other gym.  I went in and signed up.  Sara stayed in the car, well hidden behind her sunglasses and with a large coffee.

It was a long day, and by the end Julio hadn't shown up at my gym.  Sara and I drove over to Pedro's place. The boy was nowhere to be found.

I told Sara.  She said, "Do you think he quit on us?"

"No, I don't.  I think we should wait here."

Twilight was falling when I spotted Pedro ambling down the street from the south.  He hurried up when he spotted us in the car.

When he clambered into the back seat, I asked, "Where have you been?"

"I saw such a man. It was around two in the afternoon. I got on the exercise machine right next to him."

"Why?" I asked.

"You will see why. When he was done with his workout, he left. I followed him to a dark blue car. It was a Cedes."

Sara said, "A Mercedes."

"*Si, si,*" Pedro said. "I got the license number, but of course, I could do no more."

"Damn," I muttered, slapping my forehead. "I should have gotten you a cellphone."

Sara said, "Too late to worry about that now. All we can do is wait till tomorrow."

"That'll give us only a day."

She said nothing. Pedro's eyes roamed from me to Sara and back.

Suddenly Pedro dashed off back into the gym. I followed. He approached the desk guy and, looking worried, said, "Hey, mister, *mi tio*—uh, my uncle, he leave without me. He forgot he was suppose to give me a ride home."

The clerk looked at him. "Didn't you just sign up today?"

"*Si.* My uncle give me the money."

"The big guy?"

"*Si.* Could you call him, ask him to come back and get me?"

"I don't know, kid. I'm busy."

Pedro looked stricken. "*Please,* mister?"

The clerk looked at him, shrugged, and tried to go back to work.

Pedro kept up his whining and pleading until the guy turned to him and said, "Don't you know his number?"

"We staying at a motel. I don't remember. *Please*, mister. I don't want to be out here all night."

The guy finally pulled a card from his file. "Here, kid. Now, please, I'm busy, okay?"

Pedro wrote down the number and joined me in the lobby. Pedro grinned and told me what he'd done. From a phone booth in the lobby, I dialed the number. Someone answered, "Starlight Motel. Can I help you?" I promptly hung up.

The place was about five blocks north.

CHAPTER **19**

I HAD SOME CHINESE food sent to our room, and we ate. I didn't want Pedro to go ahead blindly. "I know you're wondering what this is all about," I told him. "And I'm going to tell you. But first I want you to know that I appreciate your help, and your loyalty. You may not want to go on with us. If you don't, I don't blame you, *sabes?*"

I outlined what was probably going to happen. At most, we had another day.

He looked at me wide-eyed. "*Ay, es mal! Es muy mal.*" He crossed himself. "These people are of the devil."

"That they are, my friend." I shot a glance at Sara. I knew her main motivation was to get Julio off her back, even if she had to kill him——I wasn't so caught up in the romance that I couldn't see it. Still, love is a powerful thing. It overlooks whatever it wants to.

She said, "We already know we can't just call the cops, for several reasons."

I said, "What if we call the cops and tell them there's a drug deal going on?"

She offered a tepid smile. "I told you already—it doesn't work that way. They'd be running around all over the place if they followed every unsubstantiated lead. This is a drug town. The whole police department would be tied up all the time."

"You think they have the gas in that motel room?"

"Either that or the car. They'll need it for the job. I don't know how they plan to package it exactly. I never knew any of their actual plans. They were going to tell me at that meeting."

"Then that's it," I said. "We have to get into the motel room and find it. I doubt if it's in place already. Wouldn't that be too risky?"

"Yeah, I think so."

I was fiddling with a napkin, folding it into a smaller and smaller square. "Could we just go up to the door and when they open, force our way in?"

She shook her head. "One weapon to four or five? And they won't just let you *in*. They'll kill you before you could make a move."

I took another mouthful of sub gum chow mein. "If we could get into the unit next door," I said, "I could cut through the bathroom and get into their bathroom. That would be the perfect way to surprise them. If we can get the gas, that's it." I turned to Pedro, who was unsurprisingly wide-eyed. "Do you want to go back to the garage?"

"No."

I nodded gravely, wondering if I wanted to risk the kid's life even if he didn't mind. He was only a boy. He said, "This is a wonderful country. This thing should not happen to the people." He had said it with such sincerity and honesty that I had to admire him. Right or wrong, he believed what he said.

I simply said, "Okay, *amigo*. But promise that you'll do everything I say, exactly like I say it, as if you were a soldier. Is that clear?"

"*Si, si.*"

"Okay, let's get some sleep. Tomorrow is a big day."

Sara and I slept in one bed and Pedro the other. In the morning I had trouble waking him. When he did arise, sleepy and yawning, he said, "*Ay*, that bed was comfortable. It felt so good."

Our first stop was a hardware store, where I bought a wide-toothed saw, a couple of pry bars, a coil of rope, and duct tape. Meanwhile, Sara bought herself a black, short-haired wig.

When we pulled up at the Starlight Motel, the Mercedes was parked in front of Unit 17. I pulled the car up to the office. Sara said, "Leave this to me. We can do it from 16 or 18."

She went in and started flirting with the young clerk. Five minutes later she came out, key in hand. "I told him 16 was kinda special to us and could we have it. He told me it was going to be occupied."

"Then how did you get it?"

"Two hundred bucks buys a lot of incentive. Besides, he's a sucker for romance," she added with a callous edge to her voice I didn't like. "Let's go," she said, "before they make us."

We settled inside the room. The following day would be the ninetieth anniversary of Zapata's march. Members of the Frente Revolucionario all over Mexico would celebrate. And in Los Angeles, an exiled Frente fanatic would try to kill thousands of people on the L.A. subway.

I checked out the electrical outlets. The only ones were on the other side of the room, so we wouldn't cut any wires when we went through the wall.

Speaking in whispers, I told Pedro, "We won't be able to hammer or make any noise. The idea is to poke some holes about four feet high, then slowly and quietly saw downward until we have an opening about three by four."

We turned up the TV to cover any noise. When we had the holes in and sawed down a little we found it was easier to break off six square inches of drywall at a time. We could do it with our hands. It didn't take long to get through our wall and expose the back of theirs, nailed to the two-by-fours at sixteen inch intervals, too narrow to squeeze through, so we sawed one out, which then would give us access. Luckily there was no insulation between the walls. Thank God for cheap construction. I said, "We'll wait till tonight, when they're asleep, to cut through their side."

At about eight, two men got into the Mercedes and left. Peeking through the blinds, Sara identified one of them as Julio. I said, "Maybe it's better if we break in now and wait for them. If we wait till they're asleep, they might hear us coming through the wall."

"What if they don't come *back* tonight?" Sara said.

"Then the game is up anyway." It was a nonchalant remark, but lives did depend on what we did, and that was an odd feeling for a poor man from El Salvador. All I'd ever had to look out for before was my family. But then, I wasn't alone. I had Pedro. I still had no idea where Sara's heart was.

Pedro and I broke through the wall in minutes, and all three of us swarmed over the room. But there was no Sarin gas. *"Damn!"* I shouted. "Now we have to do it the hard way."

Pedro looked at me. "What's that?"

Sara said, "Wait for them and make them tell us where it is."

It was nerve-wracking, having no idea if or when they would return. I was going to hide in the bathroom and, when they came in, get the drop on them. Sara and Pedro were to wait in our room.

By eleven that night I was so jittery I couldn't control myself, jumping at every light of every car that passed, especially when the motel guests pulled up to their units.

The Mercedes finally pulled up about one in the morning, headlights filling the room with bright light and shadow, making me feel like a rat in a trap. I slipped into the bathroom and motioned Sara and Pedro to get back. When the door opened and the light came on, I could see Julio and another guy through the cracked doorway. With my heart thumping in my chest, I burst out, leveled my weapon at them, and yelled, "Don't move! Make one move, and I'll *kill* you!"

Sara and Pedro joined me. While I kept my weapon aimed at them, Sara relieved them of theirs, carried in under-arm holsters. She kept one and handed the other to Pedro, who accepted it with a look of delight.

Confused, Julio turned his head to Sara and hissed, "What do you think you're *doing*, bitch? I have no more money. *You* have it all."

I said, "We don't care about that. I want to know where the gas is."

"*What?*"

Pedro brought out the rope. We had already cut it into convenient lengths. While I kept them covered, Sara and Julio sat them in motel chairs and tied them tightly.

My heart finally quieted down. It appeared that the situation was developing in our favor, at least for the moment. I paced back and forth before them, the gun hanging by my side. I said, "Now, let me make myself clear. I want to know what subway station the gas has been installed in. I want to know exactly where in the station it is. And if I don't find out, you are going to die." I aimed my gun directly at Julio's forehead from a distance of two feet and, trying to look menacing, spat, "Tell me. The station, and how do you plan to do it."

Julio smirked. "Do you think you frighten me, punk? I am a revolutionary. You don't scare me. Anyways, you don't look like you have the cajones to pull that trigger."

I cocked the weapon, moved closer, and pressed it against his head. His grin only grew. I said, "Your life means nothing to me."

He didn't even flinch. "Go ahead, man. Do it."

I stood him up and duck-walked him into the bathroom. Then I came back for a pillow. In the bathroom, I duct taped his mouth.

Then I said, loud enough for the other guy to hear, "I'm going to count to five. If you don't tell me, say goodbye to this world. One. . .two. . .three. . .four. . .*five*." I waited another second, took the pillow and fired twice into it. Then I came out.

Glaring at the other guy, who was looking pretty scared, I snarled, "You going to be next, *amigo*? Is it worth it to you?"

His Adam's apple was bobbing and sweat broke out on his forehead. I aimed the gun at his forehead. "*Talk*, dammit!"

The guy swallowed hard and started blubbering. "It-It's in the Seventh Street station."

"The one near Pershing Civic Center?" Sara asked.

"That's it," the man said. "The n-next stop on the line's McArthur Park. There's an engineer with us who's going to put it in the ventilation system."

"Where's the gas now?"

"In t-the machinery room, hooked up to the main blower. He's going to meet us there in the morning, and they're going to do it."

"What time?"

"Six this morning."

"Do you know where the machinery room is? Is that where the ventilation equipment is?"

"Yes, but you won't be able to get in. The subway people, they've been bribed. They'll only let Julio in."

"Yeah, well, you let me worry about that. What time will the engineer get there?"

"About three, to set everything up."

It was after two.

I got Julio out of the bathroom.  When the other guy saw he was still alive, he couldn't look him in the eye.  We taped his mouth too, and walked them out.  I said, "I think it'll be better if we use his car," so we piled into the Mercedes and put them in the back seat.  Pedro got in back with them, and Sara got in front, with her weapon trained on them.

We set out for the train station.  I took Pedro's baseball cap off his head and put it on Julio, turning the brim down low to shade and cover his face.  I did the same with my cap for his partner.  We passed a couple of police cars, one was parked on the street in front of an all-night diner, the other cruising slowly.  I kept my speed down and my driving perfect, eyes straight ahead as they stared at us.

It was a heart-pounding trip.  When we got there, I couldn't tell that it was a subway station with that upswept cupola over the entrance.  I said to the second man, "I'm going to untie you and take off the tape. You make one move to give us up, I'll blow you away, you hear me?" I turned to Pedro. "Come with me."

I left Sara in the car with Julio but pulled the .32 from her shoulder bag first.  She looked at me in surprise.  "We need him alive," I said.

With Julio's gun in my pocket, I told the other guy, "Take me to the machinery room."

We descended a flight of stairs to the station platform.  The subway had an odd smell that I remembered from when I was a kid in Union City, New Jersey, when Poppa and I took a bus into Manhattan, then the subway to his friend's house in Brooklyn.  The smell seemed to be coming from the bowels of the earth. I didn't like it. I was a country person who was used to fresh air.

When we got to the toll booth, a train was arriving, and the screech and squeal of brakes were unnerving. I had Pedro pay for all three of us. There were few people at the station, and no Metro cops in sight. The inbound train, which had just embarked a few passengers, went roaring into the dark tunnel.

We passed a couple of street people asleep on the benches who had no way of knowing that, if we weren't successful, their lives, miserable as they were, would be over. The machinery room door was locked. I knocked. There was no answer. I knocked again.

Someone said, "Who is it?"

I stood right at the door jamb and said, "Julio. Let me in."

The door opened a crack, and I jammed my gun in the doorway. "Open it, damn it."

I put my shoulder to the door and shoved it open. We dragged Julio's man in with us. When the tall guy got a look at us, he knew something was wrong. "What—"

"A little change in plans," I said, pushing him back against an inside wall. I closed the door, and Pedro and I leveled weapons at him. I said, "Where's the gas?"

He stood there looking dumbfounded.

I said, "Look, if I have to kill you, I will. Think about it. Instead of spending all that lovely money you got, you'll die right here. If you show me, I don't care about you. I'll let you go."

His eyes darting about like a frightened deer, he led me to a cylinder of gas that had a round metal unit fixed to it. "Timer?" I said.

He nodded.

I said, "Unhook it."

Hands shaking, he set to work with a screwdriver and a pair of needle-nose pliers, and in a few minutes the device was free.

I said, "Is this safe to carry?"

He said, "It's sealed.  Seal would come off when the timer releases it into the main ventilation shaft."

"Okay, then, let's see if it's really safe. You carry it upstairs to my car."

The four of us started out for the subway stairwell, getting only a couple of curious glances from the few customers.  At the curb, I was happy to see that Julio was still alive and that the car was still there.  I had no idea how Sara might react.  I knew she wanted Julio dead.  I took the cylinder from the engineer and let him and the henchman go.  They both hurried off in opposite directions.

We got into the car, and I told Sara to drive.  She said, "That's it, that's the gas I sold him."

I said, "It sure is."  I saw a police station down the street to the left.  "Drive there."

She said, "Why?"

"I'm leaving him there."  I scribbled a note to the police, stuck it in Julio's upper pocket, sticking out obviously, and shoved the cylinder under his belt.  It was a tight enough fit to hold it secure. When we got there I got out and, holding him by the arm, pulled up the hood of my windbreaker, walked him up the stairs, and shoved him through the door into the lobby.  Behind a wall of glass sat an older police officer with sergeant's stripes on his sleeve and what looked like drool on the corner of his mouth. It was early in the morning but late at night for him. He looked deep asleep, his head hanging in the chair. When I turned to leave, I was shocked to see Sara standing there behind me, a weapon in her hand. She leveled it. I shouted, "No. No." But she fired twice, dropping Julio on the police station floor. It looked like she'd shot him in the head, his blood splattered on the wall.

We both dashed to the car and sped off. Again my heart was pounding like a jackhammer. Sara seemed calm. Pedro, shaking, was mumbling, "I'm sorry, man, she took the gun from me. I wasn't expecting it."

I knew how; just how. I'd seen her deal with men too often by then.

It didn't take us long to get to the motel. Inside, we threw ourselves on the beds. I turned to her. "Why did you *do* that? You committed *murder*."

"Bull," she said. "*He* was the murderer, about to kill thousands of people. Besides, I don't want to live the rest of my life waiting for him to catch up with me. You saw him. You saw his eyes. He would never quit till he got me. So now he's gone to where all the nut jobs go, and lots of people are not going to die this morning."

I couldn't find the words to respond.

I paced around the room for nearly twenty minutes, but I couldn't escape my first thought: *We were doomed*. We'd gotten the jump on a sleepy desk sergeant and out of there pretty easily and before being detected, at least I hoped. Sara's black wig covered most of her face. The subway engineer, that was another story altogether. He could easily play the victim. I figured, though, if my note made sense to the cops, Julio would be blamed.

I tossed Pedro the keys to the Mercedes. "Load our stuff."

And then there was Sara. She was fast with the trigger, and I wondered if she had loyalties to anyone in this world but her kid sister and herself. And while I was repelled by the idea of shooting Julio like that, it did make sense, had a strong smell of justice. And he deserved it.

But I wondered if she was right, and, raised with teachings of the Lord, I knew, when her time would come, she would have some explaining to do, or would she? I wondered if the executioner got some sort of a pass. Was there such a thing as justifiable homicide in the Lord's eyes, and if so, would this fit the guidelines?

She sensed what I was thinking. "Look," she said. "You have no criminal record here. They have no prints, and we were pretty well covered, me with the wig and you with the hood. So even if there were cameras, I don't think they could identify us. But we would need a lot of luck if they didn't make me in Vegas either. And the car. That can be traced."

I'd forgotten I had unzipped the hood from the windbreaker and covered most of my face with it.

"The guns," I said. "If we're found with the guns, we'll be tied to Julio and God knows what else he and his henchman had already done."

"Then we'll only keep one," she said. "Trust me, it'll be okay."

I wanted to believe her.  I wanted everything to just go away. But all I could think about was spending the rest of my life in jail. Every minute that went by was another minute closer to being arrested by the police.  I knew they would go to great lengths to nail anybody who committed murder in the lobby of a police precinct. In a short time my entire life, crazy as it was, was going to implode, and my mother's fate be sealed.

CHAPTER **20**

**W**E SWITCHED MOTELS OUT of sensible paranoia and, with no plans, simply hung out and let our nerves loosen a bit. But they didn't. We spent a restless night. Pedro seemed to sleep. He could sleep anywhere, anytime.

Next morning I wanted to talk to Sara privately, so I sent Pedro out for food. "Since Dustin knows you want to open a restaurant in San Francisco, won't he come looking for you there?"

". . .Yeah, he would. Didn't really think of it till now."

I was hesitant to say what was on my mind, since I'd always been a coward, and a coward hates rejection, avoids it at all costs. Finally, I said, "With my money, I want to expand my farm, modernize it, make it a profitable company."

"Great idea."

"What would you, uh, think of opening your restaurant in San

Salvador? I don't think you'd have any trouble with the authorities. They like American investors."

She hardly seemed to think on it. "That's a great idea, and the U.S. dollar would go a long way down there. I could have a nice place. And bring Kathy down. Would that be okay?"

"Of course. So it's settled?"

"Not exactly."

"Why not?"

"How are things between us? You think I'm a murderer."

She was right. "I was brought up in the church," I admitted, "and the church says that killing is a sin."

"I know. The Lutherans aren't crazy about it either. But let me ask you this. If you were in the army, fighting in a war, and you were about to be killed by the enemy, would you kill first?"

I shrugged. "It's not the same."

"Why not? People fight little personal wars all the time. War doesn't have to be declared in the newspapers. The principle of war between countries is the same as war between people. You tell me—what's the difference? Some kill their enemies or anyone they see wishes them harm, without guilt. I did it for self-preservation, for me and my sister. And maybe even for you and Pedro."

"What about Vegas? That cop?"

"I was out of my mind with fear. It wasn't the same as Julio. I was so afraid of winding up in jail and Kathy having to fend for *herself*. And, thank God, the cop didn't die. He wasn't hit bad. But, again, I was thinking of my sister."

"What about the other guys in Vegas? You shot both of them?

"Emilio, you know that he would have killed you. And even then I was thinking of Kathy."

"Kathy is an adult, isn't she?"

"That's not how *I* think of her. I've been looking after her since we lost our parents, and she was a kid. She's an adult. But needy. Life's made her that way. If it'd been different, she might have turned out different. I don't know. All I know is she's what she is, and I am, too. I need to take care of her until she's ready to fly solo."

I gazed at her, and we seemed to look deeper into each other's eyes than usual. I said, "I don't mean to be judgmental, but it's important to me how I see you."

"Can I ask why?"

"Because I'm very much in love with you."

She looked startled, then threw herself into my arms, sobbing softly. We hugged, and she remained in my arms for a long while. That's how Pedro found us. He came in and avoided us as he put the food down.

While something had been settled between us, in reality nothing had. I still felt the same way about killing. But it was as if I had no choice. I was so in love with her, I knew it wouldn't matter. I wanted to be with her no matter what.

I turned to the boy. "Pedro, Sara and I have decided to go to El Salvador. I'm going to modernize my coffee farm, and she wants to open a restaurant. What do you say? Isn't it time for you to go home, too?"

He dropped his eyes, looking sad. "I will miss you guys."

"Why can't you come?"

"I still need to make money. Nothing has changed. It's even worse now, with my father gone. My mother has only me. And sometimes, the way things are going, I think that by counting on me she don't have much of a chance."

". . .Would you work for me on my farm? I'd find something other than manual labor for you, with a good salary. How does that sound?"

Slowly he looked up. "You would? A steady job?" For a moment he looked like he was going to cry. Then he hugged me and gravely said, "I am with you, *mi amigo*." When he turned away, I could see that he was holding back a sob.

We all got into the mood and had a happy lunch, toasting ourselves as the *Three Caballeros* with our sodas. After lunch we packed up and headed for Tucson for an ID for Pedro.

Pedro's phony ID identified him as my nephew Pedro Alfaro. I liked the idea. I had come to like taking care of and providing for him. I think it did as much for my paternalism as my altruism, and in some odd way put me in line with Sara's need to care for her kid sister. At least, I thought, *we have something in common.*

In Nogales, Mexico, we didn't check into our usual crummy motel but rather, in an expansive mood, the best hotel in town— not exactly five-star accommodations in Nogales, but better than our usual. And that night we again celebrated with the hotel's best dinner and champagne. I let Pedro have a sip. It made him feel adult, and he seemed to appreciate it.

## Phoenix, Morning

Dustin was sipping coffee in a local coffee shop, the *L.A. Times* before him. He frowned as he read. Finishing his coffee, he threw some money down on the counter and limped off.

At his apartment he settled himself in front of his computer and read the Las Vegas *Chronicle,* and his face twisted into a grimace. So, she still had the wetback with her, he thought. Double-crossing bitch. If he hadn't wanted his money out of her, he'd give the cops an anonymous tip, identify her, and see if *she* liked doing a stretch.

An hour later he packed a carryall, checked the load on his Smith and Wesson, packed it too, and went down to his car.

His lips were tight as he set out. His eyes, small anyway, almost blinded by hate, had shrunk even further. It was early afternoon when he spotted the sign, *Arizona State University Two Miles Ahead*, and another few minutes before he turned into the university drive.

When Kathy entered her dorm room, arms full of books, he startled her, and she dropped the books. He was sitting astride a kitchen chair facing the door, the black revolver held loosely in his hand but pointed at her. "Shut the door," he said.

Her eyes dilated with fear, but she closed the door.

He said, "You remember me? I'm Sara's friend."

"Why did you break into my room?"

"I don't think I broke in. I'm just paying a friendly visit. Relax." They traded a blank stare until he again spoke. "Don't waste my time lying to me. I want to know where Sara is."

Her eyes flashed wildly. "I-I don't know."

He grinned.  It was a most unpleasant grin.  "Didn't I just tell you not to lie to me?  I know she wouldn't keep you guessing.  I want to know where she is."

"Prob—uh, probably on her way to San Francisco.  That's what she was planning to do."

"I don't think so.  She's too hot now.  She's been a busy little girl."

Kathy did some thinking and then, hands trembling, she reached into her pocketbook.  He stiffened and trained the Smith and Wesson on her.  She pulled out a slip of paper and handed it to him.  His grin widened as he took it, read it, aimed the gun at her, and fired.  In the small room, the .40 sounded like a cannon.  The girl fell to the floor, clutching her temple.

He was gone like a phantom.

CHAPTER **21**

**W**E TRAVELED DOWN THE road feeling pretty good. The more of Mexico that went by, the closer we were getting to El Salvador. We had spent the previous evening at the El Presidente in Mexico City, spoiled by the wonderful amenities we were becoming accustomed to—gourmet dining, luxurious rooms with whirlpool baths, top-of-the-line room service. Pedro had his own room complete with cable and American TV, and he was thoroughly enjoying it.

"Hey," Sara said. "how would you guys like to really chill out? Maybe do some deep sea fishing? We're in no particular hurry now. Are we?"

Pedro and I exchanged a glance. I said to him, "What do you think?"

He said, "Yeah, man!" Still a kid, he'd have to come along with us, but I liked including him in such decisions, to make him feel, and me, too, that he was part of a family.

"Where to?" I said.

"You'll see," she said, and turned off at the next exit. The signs soon gave her away. We were turning west toward the coast, heading for Acapulco.

By noon, we had rounded a bend and begun descending toward glittering Acapulco Bay. We checked into the best hotel on the beach.

All rooms had a sea view, and ours had a terrace, too. This place wasn't called the Mexican Riviera for nothing.

We had lunch on our terrace—grouper, deliciously cooked in some kind of sauce with vegetables, a huge salad, and a bottle of Mexican wine. The taste reminded me of Momma's cooking. We had a panoramic view of the sparkling green water of the bay and the surrounding mountains, the high cliffs off to the east.

After lunch, we bought Pedro a pair of trunks at the hotel shop, got into our swimsuits, and went down to the beach. Sara, who couldn't resist the urge to buy herself a new one too, was wearing a lime-green bikini that turned most male heads we passed on the way. While we found lounge chairs to stretch out, Pedro hit the water like a fifty-caliber. We watched him dash down the sugar white beach, dance over the foaming surf, and plunge in.

I turned to her. She had stretched out and seemed truly relaxed for the first time since I met her. Her breathing was slow and steady, her breasts rising and falling. A slight smile creased the corners of her full bee-stung lips. It was a wonderful sight. She sighed and took my hand. "Just what we need," she whispered, her eyes half closed. A beach boy came by and, with an appreciative glance at Sara, asked if we'd like a drink. Though it was early, we ordered a couple of pina coladas. I was getting used to people looking at her.

She was so beautiful that, although the beach was full of attractive women, most men gave her a glance—those with women, a guarded glance, and the single ones an open one. I couldn't blame them. I was both proud and jealous, but more proud.

I would have to get used to having such a woman. In my world, what were the chances that I would have such a woman? But I knew I should value her for more than her looks, and, as usual, my feelings about this woman were mixed.

What was so different about her? Of course, if I was honest, she did have a criminal bent. She wasn't about to chase her dream in the usual way—work hard and save. I saw something else beyond that, something that I admired. People like Julio obviously had physical courage—even Arturo had physical courage, willing as he had been to go into that ranch house. Maybe even Dustin had physical courage, but it was more than that. It was the ability to *use* that courage to take care of someone other than yourself. She didn't see courage in the pursuit of self-preservation the same as the courage it took to do it for someone else.

When it finally came to me, it wasn't a shock. I had known it all along but, of course, being who I was, I didn't want to admit it. In my culture, the woman is the delicate flower who needs to be taken care of by the macho male. What would any Latino think of a situation in which the opposite was true, the woman tough and the man a shrinking violet, unable to do the distasteful things that needed to be done to survive?

It came to me in a blinding, revealing light. *Her courage.* That's what it was. I admired her courage. She not only had courage, but she was tough and competent too, qualities I wanted but didn't have. It was an odd feeling, being jealous of a woman for that. But like everything else about Sara, I needed her, and I would take her any way I could. Of course, this made me feel needy, but I couldn't help it.

And her toughness wasn't only physical. She had mental toughness, too. She did what she had to do without flinching. If I were to try to emulate her, I'd be hesitant and indecisive. I knew I would. I didn't have the mental fortitude or the strength of my convictions. She did. She fought for her own like a mother lion. Nobody would mess with her cub, and if they did, they would die for it.

In the morning, over breakfast on our terrace, Sara said, "I'm going to treat myself to a spa day."

I looked at her blankly.

"I'm going to have a massage, facial, mud bath, pedicure, manicure, and probably a hair cut."

I grinned.

"Yeah. I'm going to rebuild from the bottom up. And you guys are booked on the *Acapulco Princess* down at the Marina for a day of deep-sea fishing. It's all arranged."

"Why do I feel that you're getting rid of us?" I asked, grinning.

"Actually, I am. A girl can't have a nice spa day with guys hanging around asking dumb questions about facials and mud baths and the rest."

"I'd rather be fishing, myself."

"Me, too," Pedro added.

I gave her a kiss, found Pedro, and hurried to the Marina. While I was excited, I felt guilty, too. Here I was heading off in a recreational mood when I needed to be home. But the days spent on the open highways had affected me more than I expected. I needed a break. I just needed to relax.

We found the *Princess,* a sleek 36-foot sports cruiser, docked amid a forest of masts.

There were only the two of us aboard. The skipper was a pleasant, broad-beamed Mexican guy named Carlos, who had a set of beautifully white teeth that contrasted sharply with his deep reddish tan, and who seemed genuinely happy to have us aboard. He had a single crewman, a little wiry guy named Manuel.

About forty miles out, my fishing pole bent like a bow.

I grabbed it, raised the tension on the reel to make him pay for unwinding it, and held on with all my strength.

Carlos called out, "Pedro, back up. Give him room."

He did, and the twin engines slowed, turning gradually to keep the fish behind us. Manuel tugged at my safety harness. "Tight, man, give it everything," he whispered in my ear.

The fish wouldn't budge. I hauled up on the pole and quickly took in some line but had to pay it back out to avoid snapping it. I broke into a sweat and felt it running down my back and into the top of my shorts.

After an hour of this, letting the line run and then reeling it in what felt like a hundred times, he suddenly broke the surface through our wake—a marlin, its bill piercing the sky, its dorsal fin and scales glittering blue and gray and faint pink in the sun.

I shouted, "It's beating me, man!" The muscles on my shoulder bulged, my wrists straining as the sweat poured off my olive skin. My forearms were burning in pain, my fingers going numb—but I felt something else in my belly, something very old and hard and willed, as if this fish and I were the only living things in that whole vast sea, and one of us would have to die. I breathed in through my nose, filled my chest, and muttered, "No. It won't. I won't."

Pedro wanted to help, but Manuel motioned for him to stand back. Manuel had his arms around my waist by then, anchoring me to the chair. He pointed to a bucket of ice and water, "Pour it down his back," he shouted to Pedro. The cold water tore at my flesh. I screamed, but it woke me up.

It took two and a half hours to land it. It fought me almost the whole way before giving up ten feet from the boat, and as I hauled it in over the transom and onto the deck, I watched the faint pink and bright blue highlights of him fade to gray, and looked into the huge black eye, and knew that something in me had given way, that. . .it sounded strange to even think it, but that I could breathe for maybe the first time in my life.

I wouldn't have felt it, I suspect, if Pedro hadn't been there. He was grinning from ear to ear, though he had only caught a couple sand sharks and grouper, but he didn't care. He thoroughly enjoyed the sea and sun and the wind in his hair. Carlos fished out a bottle of a harsh red wine to celebrate, and we had a toast, Pedro taking only a few sips.

The sun was setting like a giant basketball near the horizon when we headed back to port, followed by a cloud of squealing, squawking gulls that dove at our wake for the remains of the chum Manuel had thrown overboard. When I felt dry land under my shoes, it seemed as if I was rooted to it, like a tree, and taller.

I wasn't surprised when I couldn't find Sara, figured she was probably still at the spa—but I checked there, the beach, and the pool, and I felt a pain at the base of my neck, like a little knife digging.

When I got back to the room, the phone rang. It wasn't Sara. "Okay, wetback. I've got her. I want the money, or she ends your little vacation right here."

". . .How—"

"Easy. You left a paper trail anyone could follow."

I ignored his bragging and said, "Where do you want me to meet you?"

"There's a little cove a couple hundred yards up the beach to the north. There."

"No way."

"What'd you say?"

"Too secluded, *hombre*. Too easy to kill us. No, it'll have to be on the terrace, on the level closest the beach. I need a more public place."

". . .Well," he finally said, "so our little Sara's rubbed off on you some. You seem to've grown some balls since I saw you last.  Okay, wetback.  Have it your way.  We'll be there in an hour."

He was more right than he knew—she had.

I hurried down to the desk and retrieved the suitcase from the hotel safe.  I took it back to the room, where I slipped the automatic into my waistband and bloused my shirt over it.  I clicked open the suitcase and made a few quick adjustments before I made my way to the terrace.

Dustin was already there when I showed up, sitting on an upright deck chair with a newspaper on his lap.  I knew that he had a gun under it.  Sara was sitting beside and a bit to the front of him, looking more concerned than scared.

When she saw me, she said, "Bastard surprised me."

I nodded and handed him the suitcase.  People were lingering about, having drinks.  He opened it about six inches, peeked in, and said, "I believe this concludes our transaction."  He got up and looked at Sara.  "See you in hell, babe."

He strolled off.  I fingered my gun until he was out of sight.

"I'm sorry," she murmured.  "But he isn't going to keep it."

"That's true," I said, grinning.

"What?  What do you mean?"

"He only has a few thousand.  And a lot of newspaper.  He won't find out until he stops to count it."

She said, "He's going to be wild.  He'll come back for us."

"Let him.  We'll be ready now.  And it's two to one.  He'll have to have eyes in back of his head to get us both."

Her eyes studied me anew, and I was pleased to see that she seemed happy by what she saw.

A few moments passed before she blanched right through her tan. "How did he know where we were headed?"

I shrugged. "Lucky guess?"

"No way. He doesn't know where *you're* from. How could he guess that? No. He *knew*—and there's only one way he could've."

". . .Oh, my god."

"I have to get to a phone."

I trailed her to the booth in the lobby. She was moving so fast she almost left me behind. She got on the phone while I waited.

When she again turned to me, she had turned even paler. "He *shot* her. The bastard *shot* Kathy!"

"Shit!"

"She's okay. He nearly missed—mostly powder burn. She'll be out of the hospital in the morning. But I told her not to think about coming down here until I call her."

"*Dios mio!. . .*the only hostages he can get now are Momma and Poppa. He'll head straight for the farm."

She sighed, laid a hand on my arm, and said, "Whatever we do, he's going to beat us there, so we might as well start out in the morning. He won't be a threat to anybody before he gets the money. They'll be safe until we get there."

CHAPTER **22**

**W**E WERE ON THE road before sunup.  We stopped for breakfast burritos and strong Mexican coffee, which was hard to get down, but we needed it as we hadn't gotten much sleep during the night.

El Salvador was five hundred miles away.  "We should make it by tonight."

Pedro said, "*Si*, but when we get there, the back roads in El Salvador are not so good.  It will slow us down."

"You're right," I said.

Sure enough, we were.  In the twilight, I hit a rock or something and tore loose a tie rod.  No matter what I did, the wheels only spun us around in a circle.  After examining the front end I said, "The last sign said there was a village up ahead.  Pedro, it would be best if you went on ahead for help and we waited here with the car.  A new car like this might tempt somebody to tow it away."

"*Si*," he said, and set off.

Sara lit a cigarette, took a drag, and handed it to me. "Take it easy. I don't think we're going anywhere tonight."

Pedro didn't come back in the tow truck. When I asked the driver where he was, the man shrugged. It was odd.

He towed the car to the village, nothing more than the garage and maybe a dozen other buildings on the main road. Pedro was nowhere to be found.

The garage man told us he would have to send for the part. The car would be tied up for days. And there didn't seem to be any direct transportation anywhere.

My stomach was tying itself in knots when I spotted an 88 Pontiac Trans Am parked on the side. I asked, "Whose car is that?"

"Mine," said the garage man.

"Would you sell it?"

"Oh, no, *Signor*. I need transportation."

"Would you take three thousand US?" I knew it was worth no more than three hundred.

His eyes lit up. "*Tres mil? US?*" he repeated.

"*Si*."

Twenty minutes later, we were on our way to the farm, which I estimated was about seventy-five miles off.

We got there in pitch darkness. From the edge of the nearest coffee field, I could see a dim light in the house. There was a car out front, Dustin's I figured. Sara didn't recognize it.

We crept closer for a better look. I spotted a motorcycle out front. When we were within twenty yards, the house light went off and a shotgun blast rang out, reverberating over the fields. It was answered by two quick bursts of what sounded like pistol fire. The full moon was throwing a cold luminosity over the terrain. We exchanged a quick glance. Pedro. Of course. He hadn't run out at all. Or was Poppa shooting it out with Dustin?

There were more shots, which sent my stomach into turmoil. I whispered, "Let's move up closer." When we were just about on a level with the shooter outside the house, I could see that the pistol shots were coming from behind our farm tractor, parked out front. The weapon flashed in the dim light.

I couldn't get a clear shot at him, but I figured I could get him to stop shooting at the house. I pulled out the automatic and fired twice, the loads sparking as they pinged off the tractor. The pistol fire ended. Sara whispered, "I'm going to circle around to the right."

I said, "No. What good will it do? We only have one gun."

"I could make some noise and distract him. He won't know I'm not armed, and he'll then have to be watching three people."

"*No,*" I snapped. "Too risky."

She didn't answer, but when I turned again, she was gone.

I fired several more times at intervals to distract him.

I only had one extra clip of ammunition, and I couldn't afford to engage in a long gun battle. I had to make my move. I crept closer and was within sight when I heard Sara scream. Then I saw her. Dustin was in back of her with a lock hold around her neck, which she kept pulling at. He duck-walked her to the front door of the farmhouse in such a way that neither the shooter in the house nor I could get a shot off without hitting her.

"All right," he snarled. "Enough screwing around. Give me the money, or I blow her away—and the old folks and the kid, too."

It had to be Pedro firing the shotgun.

I called out, "It's in the car, parked up near the road. I'll have to get it."

"Then go. I know where the road is. It shouldn't take more than twenty minutes there and back. If you're not back by then, I start killing people. And I'll start with our little *chiquita* here."

I yelled, "Okay."

I dropped back out of sight. I had no idea what to do.

Twenty minutes later, I still had no plan. My heart sitting on my stomach. Dustin called out, "Wetback? You out there? It's time. I'll start with the bimbo here. Or maybe I'll start with the old man. I don't know which you value more, but it makes no difference to me. . . . No," he concluded, "I changed my mind. I'm going to start with the old man. Next will be *Mamacita*."

I saw him press the muzzle to Sara's head and start for the door while she squirmed and kicked with all her might. Then I saw him haul off and knock her out with the gun butt and start for the door.

That's when I heard the scream. It was more than primeval, something out of another world, ungodly, really, inhuman. I didn't realize it was me screaming until I had charged within ten feet of Dustin. His first shot hit my shoulder. The second must have hit my leg—it dropped me to the ground. He fired again and missed, and I flung myself across the ground and around the corner of the house while he struggled with Sara, hearing an unearthly scream like that of a hawk in my ears, and it was only when I was out of sight and had the building between us that I realized it was *me* screaming again—all my frustrations, my rage and disappointment, boiling up through my vocal chords.  I dragged myself around to the other side of the house, my hands cold as ice, fingers barely able to move, enough in shock to be numb to the pain.  I only knew that I was bleeding because I could feel the wet blood.

He knew I hadn't brought the bag—he was going to have to keep me alive until he found out where it was.  I knew about the trap door in our root cellar, with the set of stairs that led to the back hallway. I dragged it open and set it back on its hinges without a creak, and slipped into the dark, making my way to the stairs at the other end through a rolling wave of haze.  My left eyelid had begun to twitch. I staggered up the stairs, pulling out the gun, clicking back the hammer, and tried the door before I remembered, through the haze that had started to grow thicker, that it was locked.  I had no choice: I put my good shoulder to it, and it gave way.

I heard Dustin rushing toward me down the long, narrow hallway from the front, a shadow, almost a mirage of fluttering grays— but I knew it was him, not Pedro or my folks, could tell from the lanky build, his height, and his limp.  My right arm was stiff, but I used my left hand to drag it chest high, the weapon appearing in front of me as if by magic, and squeezed the trigger three times and heard the blasts, sparks flying from muzzle, and a *thunk*, before something hot buzzed in my ear and the abyss drew me in. It was black, swirling, and bottomless.

# Epilogue

**T**HE SHADOWY FIGURES HOVERING above me in a circle began to re-solve into human faces. Were these the angels of death? Was I in Hell for my evil deeds?

A female voice said, "*Signor? Signor?* Are you awake?"

"Wha? What?"

"Relax." She was dressed in white and had a nurse's cap. "You are in the hospital. You've been hurt."

Then I saw Pedro, his face anxious and alarmed. "*Amigo?* You are going to be fine."

I noticed the IV in my arm. I had some kind of tube in my nose, and I was bandaged all over, my side, my thigh, and my head.

He saw the questions in my eyes. "We are all okay, *hombre.* Sara has a wound in her arm, but is not serious. *Tu mama y tu papa tam-bien.* Both of them okay."

"*You? You* were firing the shotgun?"

"*Si*, it was me. I got there just before him. I was so glad you come. I was out of shells. Your folks only had one box, and I use all of them."

I nodded. "You did good, *amigo*."

When Sara came in, he stepped back. She was about to throw herself into my arms, but the monitoring devices and IV held her back. She took my hand instead, and kissed it. "I'm so glad to see you awake, babe. I was so scared. Other than Kathy, I've never been scared for anybody."

"Dustin?"

"He's dead. You pulled the trigger three times, and one of them hit his aorta. *He* lost the war, babe." She knew I understood what she meant. And now that the shoe was on the other foot, I realized I didn't feel terrible about it. I would have felt a lot worse if Sara, Pedro, or my parents had been harmed.

We had traveled the same road, she and I, and reached the other end together. Courage was no more than doing what you absolutely had to, that no fear on earth could dissuade you from doing. Either I had taken a step closer to her, or she had taken one closer to me. All I knew, as my mother and father entered the room with smiles of thanksgiving on their faces, was that that strange tough girl and I were closer.

This book has been set in Perpetua,
designed by Eric Gill in the early part of
the 20th century; he based it on the
designs of old engravings.  His most
popular Roman typeface, it was released
by the Monotype Corporation between
1925 and 1932, first appearing in a
limited edition of the book *The Passion of
Perpetua and Felicity*, for which the typeface
was named.  The italic form was originally
called Felicity.  The formal impression
which this font lends to any text is due in
part to its small, diagonal serifs and its
medieval numbers.